# Welco... !

Gone to the stables

*Jina*

Shh!! Studying—
please do not disturb!

*Mary Beth*

<u>GO AWAY!!!</u>

*Andie*

Hey, guys!
Meet me downstairs in the
common room. Bring popcorn!

*Lauren*

Join Andie, Jina, Mary Beth, and Lauren for more fun at the Riding Academy!

"What are we looking for?" Lauren asked in a low voice.

"Evidence," Mary Beth whispered back. She shined her flashlight around the dark room.

"Let's start over there." She went over to a small rolltop desk, where a notebook was lying open on the blotter. The top of the page was dated January 3.

"That's today's date," Mary Beth said excitedly as she aimed the light on the page. "This must be a journal of some kind."

Suddenly, she heard the sound of footsteps coming closer.

Beside her, Lauren gasped.

"Quick, we've got to hide," Mary Beth hissed to her friend. "Somebody's coming!"

Super Special
1

# HAUNTED
# HORSEBACK
# HOLIDAY

by Alison Hart

Library of Congress Catalog Card Number: 96-70630

ISBN: 0-679-88053-9

RL: 4.5

Tinted in the United States of America

10 9 8 7 6 5 4 3 2 1

BULLSEYE BOOKS

Random House New York

1

"I think I'm going to be sick."

Andie Perez glanced up from the *Horse and Rider* magazine she was reading. In the plane seat next to her, Mary Beth Finney, one of her roommates from Foxhall Academy, was doubled over.

"How can you be sick already?" Andie knew Mary Beth was worried about her first plane ride, but they hadn't even taken off yet.

"It's the propellers. They're shaking the plane," Mary Beth moaned. Her auburn bangs stuck to her damp forehead, and her red freckles were tinged with green.

"Propellers?" Andie couldn't believe her roommate was so dumb. "Jets don't have propellers. Streams of air or gas or something spurt out of the motors."

1

Mary Beth groaned. "That's even worse!"

"Finney, you're a real pain." With a sigh of impatience, Andie handed her friend the throw-up bag from the compartment in front of her. "Use this. It's a long flight to Denver."

Unsnapping her seat belt, Andie stood up and leaned over the seat in front of her. Lauren and Jina, her other two roommates from Foxhall Academy, sat side by side. They were huddled together, giggling.

"Does someone want to change places with me? Finney's going to be sick."

"Eww." Lauren wrinkled her nose. She unsnapped her belt and, kneeling on the seat, looked back at Mary Beth. "Do you want a soda? That might help."

"Girls, you need to sit down and buckle your seat belts," a male flight attendant told them as he walked down the aisle.

"He's cute," Andie whispered to Lauren. Sitting down, she flipped her wild dark hair behind her shoulders and picked up her magazine again. Mary Beth was staring out the window, the throw-up bag clutched in her hand. An unopened book lay across her lap.

"Why don't you read your book?" Andie

suggested. "It'll take your mind off the flight."
She peered at the title, *The Wild West*.

"Why did you bring that? We're going to a
ski and riding resort, not back to the OK
corral."

"I know," Mary Beth said. "I just thought
it'd be fun to read about Colorado's history.
I've never been out West before."

Unzipping her fanny pack, Andie pulled
out a colorful, crumpled brochure and handed
it to her roommate. "Here."

Mary Beth read the front. "But this is for
someplace called Snow Mecca. We're going to
the White Horse Lodge."

"My mom couldn't get a brochure from the
White Horse," Andie explained. "But it's supposed to be just like Snow Mecca—except better, because we can ride."

Andie pointed to a photo of four girls skiing
down a hill wearing bright ski outfits. "See?
That's us tomorrow morning. And"—she
tapped a picture of four people soaking in a
steaming hot tub—"that will be us tomorrow
night after we've snagged a couple of hot
dates."

Mary Beth giggled. "Hot dates? You've got

to be kidding. Dorothy will be with us every second, remember? I doubt she'll let us stay up past nine o'clock."

Andie gave up. Just because Finney always expected the worst, didn't mean she had to. She was ready to *party*. She deserved it after a whole tough semester at Foxhall.

When she tucked the brochure back into her fanny pack, a postcard from Steamboat Springs fell out. It was her mother's idea of a Christmas card.

Andie turned it over and read the message: *See you soon! Hope you have a Merry Day. Love you.*

*Sure you love me. Then why weren't you with me for Christmas?*

Her dad had really tried. They'd decorated a tree, popped popcorn, and watched *Miracle on 34th Street*. He'd given her what she'd asked for—money. Added to her other savings, she was on her way to buying Mr. Magic, the Foxhall horse she was dying to own. Then, as a surprise, her dad had thrown in another present—a brand-new ski outfit for the trip.

All she'd gotten from her mom was a postcard.

*And this trip*, Andie reminded herself

quickly. Her mother had even paid for Jina, Lauren, Mary Beth, and Dorothy Germaine, Foxhall's barn manager, to go too. *It's her way of making up for not seeing me for seven months, twenty-eight days, and five hours*, Andie added to herself.

Her stomach knotted at the thought of being with her mother again. She almost reached for a throw-up bag. Then she took a deep breath.

She wasn't going to be like Finney. She was going to look on the *bright side*.

For a whole week she'd have a chance to get to know her mom again. She would swallow all her angry why-did-you-leave-me questions and make it the greatest vacation ever—even if it killed her.

"We're *not* going to crash, we're *not* going to crash," Mary Beth repeated over and over to herself as the jet raced faster and faster down the runway.

A roaring noise filled her ears. Her insides rolled, then lifted suddenly as the plane took off.

"Hey, cool!" Andie leaned across Mary Beth's lap and pointed out the window.

Mary Beth stole a quick look. Trees, roads, and houses were falling beneath her as if they were dropping into space. She let out a strangled cry.

"I thought you'd like that." Andie laughed and settled back in her seat. "Soon we'll be above the clouds. Then you won't be able to see anything except blue sky."

"Sky?" Mary Beth croaked.

"Until we land in Denver, and then we'll get on one of those tiny little planes. They crash all the time. Whack!" Andie smacked her palms together. "Instant pancake."

Bile rose in Mary Beth's throat. Swallowing hard, she flipped open her book.

*Why did I ever come on this trip?* she asked herself for the millionth time. She'd been having such a good visit with her family. For Christmas, Tammy had gotten a doll whose hair you could wash and color. Reed had gotten plastic blocks, and Benji a car racing set. She could have spent the last week of break happily playing with little sister and brothers.

Instead she was strapped inside a huge piece of metal, hurtling through space to a ski and riding resort—even though she'd never skied in her life and she was a terrible rider.

She held on to her book as if it were a life preserver. Maybe reading would help her ignore the rolling of her stomach. And, if she learned a little about Colorado's history, she could at least sightsee when they arrived.

She opened to the first page. A cowboy was being thrown from a horse. Her heart skipped a beat. She'd barely mastered posting. How was she going to ride some snorting bronc?

Quickly, she flipped through the book, stopping at a photo of a man with a handlebar mustache. CATTLE RUSTLER, the caption read.

Mary Beth nudged Andie with her elbow. "Hey, do they still have rustlers out West?"

"Definitely," Andie said, "but now they look like this." She pointed to a photo in her *Horse and Rider* magazine of a handsome cowboy wearing tight jeans and a flirtatious grin.

"Give me a break." Mary Beth shut her book.

"Hey, Finney, lighten up." Andie punched her playfully on the arm. "*I'm* planning on having a great time. Even if my mother's bringing along her dopey Italian boyfriend."

"I guess you're right." Mary Beth sighed. "I'll just think of this as a Wild West adventure."

Peering around Andie, Mary Beth checked out the plane. When she'd boarded, she'd been too nervous to notice any of the passengers. Now she focused on a man sitting in the aisle seat across from them. He wore a cowboy hat and boots.

*A real cowboy,* Mary Beth thought. If he'd lived in the Wild West, he probably would have been some famous lawman.

Suddenly, he turned his head, and Mary Beth's heart skipped a beat. He had a black mustache, whiskery chin, and a patch over one eye.

Quickly, Mary Beth opened *The Wild West* to the photo of the rustler. Except for the eye patch, the two men looked identical.

Mary Beth grabbed Andie's wrist. "Don't look now," she whispered excitedly, "but there's a cattle thief on our plane!"

2

"Sure, Mary Beth," Andie murmured without looking up from her magazine. "There's a cattle thief on the plane. And there's a bucking bronco in the baggage compartment, too."

"No, I mean it." Mary Beth jerked her thumb toward the aisle. "He's sitting right next to you. The guy with the eye patch. I wouldn't be surprised if he has a derringer tucked in his boot."

Andie looked at her, one brow arched. "A what?"

"A little gun." Mary Beth tapped *The Wild West*. "You can read all about it in here."

Andie shook her head. "You've lost it, Finney."

"Drinks, ladies?"

Mary Beth snapped her chin up. The flight

attendant was hovering over them. "Uh, yeah."

He handed them napkins, peanuts, and two small plastic glasses overflowing with soda. When he pulled the cart out of the way, Mary Beth glanced nonchalantly at the cowboy. Andie did too, taking a sip as she looked.

"Okay, so he's wearing a cowboy hat and he has a droopy mustache," she told Mary Beth as she unlatched her food tray. "That hardly makes him a bad guy. Besides, cattle rustlers hang around cows, not planes." She giggled. "Unless he's planning on stealing the beef Stroganoff we're having for lunch."

"Ha-ha." Mary Beth folded her arms. So she'd gotten a little carried away with her Wild West fantasy. At least it had helped her forget about the plane crashing.

"There they are! The Rockies!" Andie cried several hours later. After a short layover in Denver, they'd boarded a smaller plane.

"Where? Where?" Jina, Lauren, and Mary Beth chorused. This time, the girls were sitting in the same row. Lauren was beside Andie. Jina and Mary Beth were seated directly across the aisle.

Andie sat back so Lauren could peer over her shoulder.

"Wow!" Lauren gasped. "They're so snowy and sharp looking."

"And just think, right now people are down there helio-skiing. You know, where they get dropped off to ski down some big cliff. Wouldn't that be awesome?" Andie exclaimed.

Lauren shuddered. "I'll take a groomed slope with a ski lift, thank you."

"Chicken," Andie teased.

But her playful mood quickly died. The flight was almost over, and soon they'd be landing in Grand Junction. Would her mother be there to meet her?

It had been so long since Andie had seen her mother, she'd almost forgotten what she looked like. The last photo she'd sent from Europe showed her looking short and pudgy in front of the Eiffel Tower. But that had been ages ago. Now her mom skied in Steamboat Springs and had an Italian boyfriend named Alfonso.

Nervously, Andie zipped and unzipped her fanny pack as she stared out the window.

"It'll be all right, Andie." Lauren patted her arm. "We'll be having so much fun, you and

your mom won't have time to worry about anything." Lauren wiggled in her seat like a little
kid. "I can't wait to learn how to ride Western."

Suddenly, the plane started to descend.
Andie gripped the sides of her seat. She could
hear Mary Beth chattering to Jina, her voice
rising hysterically each time the plane
bounced.

Finally, the plane landed, and they taxied
into the airport. Andie gathered her coat and
carry-on bag and joined her roommates in the
crowded aisle.

"Do you see him?" Mary Beth whispered in
Andie's ear.

"Who?" Andie frowned.

"Patch. The cattle rustler, remember? He
boarded the plane for Grand Junction, too."

"Maybe he's following me. I do have a
*cow*hide suitcase." Andie burst out laughing,
way too loud. Jina and Lauren turned to stare
at her as they started down the gangway to the
terminal.

"Hey, I see someone holding up a sign that
says White Horse," Jina called.

Andie quickened her pace. Her palms were
beginning to sweat. "Is it a short woman with
bleached-blond hair?"

Just then, a man jostled Andie's arm. She looked up. It was the guy with the eye patch.

He nodded curtly, then strode through the crowd, pushing between the passengers as if he was in a big hurry. When Andie reached the end of the gangway, Jina and Lauren were waiting. Next to them stood a teenaged girl holding a poster that said, WHITE HORSE LODGE.

Andie glanced around for her mother. *Where was she?*

"Come on." Mary Beth came up beside her and surged ahead, her suitcase bumping her knees as she walked.

"Hi," the girl greeted them. "I'm Jenny. White Horse Lodge welcomes you to Grand Junction."

"Nice to meet you." Mary Beth dropped her suitcase and shook Jenny's hand. "I'm Mary Beth and I'm so glad to be back on solid ground."

Just then, an older man, and a boy about the roommates' age walked up to the group.

"Here's the rest of the welcoming committee," Jenny said with a grin. "This is Bronc." She pointed to the older man who nodded politely. He wore a denim jacket that was gray with dirt. Patchy whiskers darkened his chin, and one of his cheeks bulged.

Andie grimaced. She hoped the other cowboys she met looked a little cleaner.

"And this is Cole." Jenny pointed to the guy. "He's the son of Mr. and Mrs. McRae, the Lodge owners."

Andie turned her attention to Cole. He wore a cowboy hat, jeans, and a goose-down vest over a western-style shirt. His fingers were shoved in his pockets, and he was rocking on his boot heels with a bored expression.

Andie gave him a bored expression right back. Cole McRae was hardly her idea of a real cowboy, but at least he was clean.

"Everybody's here," Cole said to Jenny. "Mr. Delasandro is getting his luggage."

"Good." Jenny lowered the poster. "We can head on down to the baggage claim area. The Lodge is about an hour and a half drive from Grand Junction."

"Is Dorothy there already?" Lauren asked.

Jenny nodded. "Ms. Germaine arrived yesterday. She's skiing right now."

Lauren squealed and nudged Andie. "Did you hear that? *Dorothy* skiing?"

"What about my mother?" Andie asked anxiously. "Her name is—" She hesitated. What was her mother calling herself these days? "Charlotte Perez."

"Oh." Jenny gave Andie a sympathetic look. "Your mother called this morning and left a message. She said to tell you that she's terribly sorry, but she won't be coming."

"Not coming?" Andie repeated. "What do you mean, not coming? This is supposed to be our vacation together! I haven't seen her in months and now she won't even be here! Oh, that's just *great*."

Throwing up her hands, Andie glared at Jenny, Bronc, and Cole as if it were all their fault. Then she turned around so they wouldn't see her angry tears.

*Some welcoming committee,* she thought angrily.

*Where was her mother?*

Andie swiped at the tears before they spilled down her cheeks. She didn't have to show the whole world how upset she was. Squaring her shoulders, she turned back to face the group.

Jenny, Lauren, Jina, and Mary Beth stood in a circle, whispering. Bronc had wandered away and was spitting a wad of something into a trash can. The only one left was Cole, who eyed her curiously.

Andie wanted to stick her tongue out at him. Who did he think he was, anyway?

Sure, he had gorgeous blue eyes like the guy in the magazine. And he might even be cute if he wiped that smirk off his face. Not that she cared. She was too mad about her mother.

Turning, Andie tapped Jenny on the shoulder. "So why isn't my mother coming?" she demanded.

Jenny hesitated. "She is coming, Andie. Just not for a day or two. Steamboat Springs was snowed in last night. It'll take at least a day to get the mountain roads cleared."

"Oh." Relief flooded Andie's chest. *Her mother was coming after all!* "Why didn't you tell me that in the first place?"

"She would've, but you didn't give her a chance," Cole said.

Andie opened her mouth, ready to give Cole McRae a sharp retort. But before she could say anything, he picked up Lauren's overnight bag and walked off.

"This vacation is going to be so-o-o-o cool," Lauren whispered. "Can you believe it? These guys are real cowboys."

Andie snorted. "Cowboys? No way. They only dress like that for the tourists."

"Ready?" Jenny asked.

The four girls gathered up their things and followed the welcoming committee through the terminal to the baggage claim area.

Andie lagged behind. She didn't know whether to be sad or relieved that her mother wouldn't be arriving right away. Now, at least, she could quit worrying for a while about how they'd get along. She could relax and enjoy the skiing, horses, and hot tubs. And hadn't she heard things about sleigh rides, an indoor pool, and snow parties?

Quickly Andie caught up with the others. Now she was definitely glad her mom wouldn't be coming for another day. She was ready to have some major fun at White Horse Lodge.

Mary Beth giggled to herself as she walked behind Bronc. He was so bowlegged, she could see a foot of daylight between his knees. Even the seat of his jeans was dusty, as if he'd just gotten off his horse.

Then a horrible thought hit her. Why was he named Bronc? Did that mean he rode wild horses? Did that mean *she* would have to ride wild horses?

"Jenny!" Hurrying ahead, Mary Beth caught up with the older girl. "Are the resort horses gentle?"

Looking over his shoulder, Cole gave her a strange look.

Jenny shrugged. "Depends," she said as they walked under the baggage claim sign.

"But don't worry. We can find you a quiet one."

*Whew.* If Mary Beth had had a free hand, she would have wiped the sweat off her brow.

Jenny hurried over to the crowd waiting at the baggage claim. "Oh, good, the suitcases are here already. Bronc, would you help the girls get their things? Cole, will you please find Mr. Delasandro? He'll ride with you and Bronc. I'll take the girls with me."

Half an hour later, Jenny, Lauren, Andie, Mary Beth, and Jina were bouncing along in an old, extended cab pickup. Their luggage had been tossed in the truck bed. Mary Beth was crammed in the narrow backseat with Lauren, her knees drawn up around her neck. It was so cold, she'd draped her jacket over her legs.

"Wow, look at the mountains," Lauren said. Since they'd been traveling east from Grand Junction, they'd driven higher and higher with each mile.

"We don't call those mountains," Jenny corrected. "They're foothills."

"Are you from around here?" Jina asked. She was squeezed in the front between Andie and Jenny.

The older girl shook her head. She had brown hair styled in shaggy layers. And like Cole, she wore jeans and a goose-down vest. Mary Beth wondered if everyone at the resort dressed so casually. She had been expecting the latest in winter fashions.

"Will we have time for skiing when we get there?" Andie asked. Her nose was pressed against the glass as she stared out the side window at the ranches and pastures nestled at the base of the snow-covered hills.

"I doubt it," Jenny replied. "Dinner's at six sharp. You're expected to be seated at the table or you don't get served."

Mary Beth glanced at Lauren. "We all eat at the same table?" she whispered. She'd been picturing crackling logs in a stone fireplace surrounded by intimate, candlelit booths. A waiter named Claude would take their orders of filet mignon and lobster, and Henri would hover over them filling their soda glasses.

Lauren shrugged. "I guess," she whispered back. "We'll meet more people that way."

"True." Lauren had a point, Mary Beth realized. Maybe she could meet a fellow klutz to ski with on the baby slope.

Mary Beth rubbed a cramp in her thigh. In

front, Andie and Jina were asking Jenny about something. Jenny kept nodding her head, but the truck's motor made so much noise, Mary Beth couldn't hear what they were saying. Somehow, she hadn't expected a rusty truck with no heat. Shouldn't a fancy resort like White Horse at least have a van?

Just then, Jenny pointed ahead. "That's the western slope of the Rockies."

Mary Beth had to duck to see out the windshield. In the distance, jagged, snow-topped peaks rose above the foothills. Beside her, Lauren oohed and aahed. Mary Beth wished she'd brought her camera.

"And on your left is a wild horse management area."

"Wild horses!" Andie and Jina chorused.

"You mean there really are wild horses in Colorado?" Jina asked.

Jenny nodded. "Yup. White Horse Lodge is near the eastern edge of the management area, so we can ride in to see the horses if we want."

"Wow," Mary Beth murmured as she sat back again.

The truck hit a pothole as Jenny turned off the main highway onto a one-lane road. Mary

Beth jounced high, hitting her head on the roof.

Things weren't starting off so well, Mary Beth thought. She was exhausted, and her head ached. It was five-thirty Colorado time, but back home it would be eight-thirty. No wonder she was hungry.

The road turned into gravel as the truck wound higher and higher into the foothills. Mary Beth squinted out the window. All she could see was sagebrush, scrubby trees, rocks, and more hills. They seemed to stretch on forever.

She scratched her head, puzzled. Weren't most ski resorts near busy towns with posh restaurants and trendy shops?

"Uh, how much farther?" Andie asked from the front seat. Mary Beth realized she wasn't the only one wondering where they were going.

"Just around the bend," Jenny said.

Mary Beth craned her neck, trying to see. The resort must be on the side of the hill, she decided.

But when they rounded the bend, there was no fancy lodge. All Mary Beth saw was a log ranch house, a barn, two smaller buildings, and some rickety fencing.

Jenny swung the pickup in front of the ranch house. It was two stories, about the size of Mary Beth's house back in Cedarville, with a big porch.

"Here we are," Jenny said. She parked the pickup but no one moved. Lauren, Mary Beth, Andie, and Jina stared out the windows in total silence.

"This is it?" Andie asked finally.

"Yup." Jenny opened the driver's door and frigid air blasted into the truck. Mary Beth hugged her jacket to her chest.

"This is White Horse Lodge?" Andie repeated as if in shock.

"You got it." Jenny jumped out, then stuck her head in the truck. "And you have fifteen minutes to get your stuff and put it away before Mrs. McRae puts dinner on the table."

Jenny pulled the driver's seat forward so Mary Beth could get out, then ran around to the back. Still, no one moved.

"Where's the ski slope?" Lauren asked.

"And the indoor pool?" Andie added.

"And the riding arena and hot tubs," Mary

Beth wailed. She could feel herself starting to lose it. She'd risked her life in an airplane for *this?*

Jenny opened the passenger door. "Come on, girls. Grab your gear. I'll show you the bunkhouse."

"Bunkhouse?" Jina croaked as she climbed out after Andie. "We're sleeping in a bunkhouse?"

Andie was shaking her head from side to side and muttering, "This is a mistake. Just a mistake."

As Mary Beth climbed out the driver's side, a second truck pulled up and parked.

"I'll have to introduce all of you to Mr. Delasandro, our other guest," Jenny said, bustling up.

A man climbed out of the truck. He put his cowboy hat on his head, then turned toward Mary Beth. When she saw who it was, she stepped backward in alarm.

It was the Patch—cattle rustler!

4

"Uh, hi, Mr.—uh—Delasandro," Mary Beth stammered. Clutching her jacket closer to her chest, she fled around the truck.

"Andie! It's Patch. He's here at the Lodge!"

"Who cares?" Andie snapped. "We're not staying here anyway. This is all a mistake. My mother wouldn't pick a dump like this for my vacation."

Mary Beth peered nervously over her shoulder. Patch was carrying his suitcase up the steps of the ranch house.

"Well, *I* think it's a neat place," Lauren said. "Look—horses!" She pointed to a corral attached to the barn. About eight shaggy-coated horses hung their heads over the fence, Lauren dropped her bag and ran over to see them.

"Those aren't horses," Andie called after her. "They're large goats."

Jina was looking around, a shocked expression on her face. "This is a ranch, not a resort."

"Yeah, and it's sure not my idea of a primo vacation spot," Andie grumbled. "I'm calling my mother and finding out why we're in the middle of nowhere—"

"With a strange guy wearing an eye patch," Mary Beth finished breathlessly.

Andie spun to face her. "Would you quit talking about that guy? He's just some stupid guest who got suckered into coming to this dump like us."

Flushing, Mary Beth ducked her head. Andie was right. She was being dumb.

"Hey, girls, let's go," Jenny called. "Cole will show you to the bunkhouse. Then you can wash up, and head back to the main house for dinner."

Mary Beth picked up her things and followed Cole down a snow-packed path toward one of the buildings. It was a single-story version of the ranch house with two front doors. Smoke curled from a stone chimney, and icicles hung off the porch roof.

Lauren caught up with Mary Beth. "The

horses are so cute!" she gushed.

"They're yearlings," Cole said over his shoulder. Climbing the stone steps, he stomped his boots on the wooden porch.

"Jenny lives next to you in the other half of the bunkhouse," he said. He opened the door and went in, letting the door swing shut behind him.

"Such a gentleman," Andie muttered.

Mary Beth hauled her suitcase up the steps and onto the porch. It weighed a ton. If she'd known she'd be vacationing in the wilderness, she would have left her dressy clothes behind.

When Mary Beth stepped inside, Lauren was already climbing a ladder to the top of a bunk bed. "This is so cool! I haven't slept in one of these since I visited my cousins."

"I get the other top bunk." Mary Beth quickly dragged her suitcase across the room.

Andie had stopped in the doorway. Her nose was wrinkled as if she smelled something gross.

Mary Beth didn't think the place was *that* bad. A hooked rug covered the planked floor. Each bed had two fluffy pillows and a thick quilt. There was a tall dresser, a small desk, two overstuffed chairs, and a wooden rocker.

"This is so cozy!" Lauren cooed from the top of her bunk.

"It is kind of cute," Jina admitted. She'd slung her designer suitcase onto one of the lower bunks.

"White Horse Lodge has everything those fancy resorts in Aspen have," Cole said, opening the door to the bathroom. "Check out the posh facilities."

With a sweep of his arm, he gestured to the bathtub. "Fill it with hot water, swirl your fingers, and there you go—a hot tub. Later, add cold water, and—presto—a swimming pool."

He started to laugh, and Mary Beth realized he must have overheard them talking at the airport. No wonder he had looked at them so strangely.

Andie placed her hands on her hips. "I don't think that's funny."

"I do." Cole grinned. "It cracks me up to think you girls thought you were coming to some fancy place. This is a working ranch, Maryland girl."

Just then, a little boy about six years old burst into the room. "Howdy!" he greeted them. "Ma says dinner's ready."

Cole ruffled the boy's blond hair. "This

here's Nathan, the only cute guy on the place. So don't fight over him." He bit back another snort of laughter.

Andie curled her fingers, looking as if she might strangle him. Nathan just beamed at everybody. Mary Beth couldn't help smiling back. He had freckles and messy hair just like her little brother, Reed.

"So hurry and wash up," Nathan said. Then whirling around, he raced from the bunkhouse, slamming the door behind him.

Still chuckling, Cole squatted on the floor and began to throw logs into a woodstove. He'd tilted his hat back and a shock of blond hair fell over his forehead.

"I'll wash first," Jina said, heading for the bathroom.

"I'm only going to show you how to do this once, guys," Cole said. "Then it's up to you to keep the stove filled. When you open the door, make sure—"

A scream interrupted his instructions. Jina threw open the bathroom door. "There's a rat in here!"

"A rat!" Mary Beth jumped off the top bunk. "Where?" She peered into the bathroom. A brown and white mouse scurried from behind the toilet.

"Hey, that's not a rat," Cole said. "That's my brother's mouse, Binky." He snatched it up by the tail. "Nathan!" he hollered out the bunkhouse door. "Get your mouse out of here!"

"A mouse!" Andie said haughtily. "Okay, that does it." She crossed her arms. "Now I'm definitely calling my mother." Mary Beth and Lauren started to giggle.

Just then, Mary Beth saw someone walking past the open doorway of the bunkhouse. She peered out the frosty window. It was Patch. He was hunkered down in his coat, his collar pulled high around his neck as if he didn't want anyone to recognize him.

"Hey, Cole. Does Colorado still have cattle rustlers?" Mary Beth asked.

"Sure," Cole said. "Bad ones, too. They back their tractor-trailers up to the barbed wire fence, cut the wire, and herd the cattle right into the trailer."

"Oh," Mary Beth murmured. She watched Patch until he rounded the corner of the ranch house. Maybe she wasn't so dumb. Maybe Patch wasn't just a guest. He could be here checking out the cattle.

*Jina's right,* she thought. *There is a rat at White Horse Lodge.* A human rat. And Mary Beth was determined to keep her eye on him.

"But Mom, what do you *mean* you picked White Horse Lodge on purpose?" Andie protested into the phone. "This place is a dump. It barely has running water and electricity."

"Now, Andie, I'm sure that's an exaggeration," her mother said on the other end. "I talked with Dorothy Germaine earlier, and she said it was rustic but delightful."

"It's rustic, all right. Jina found a huge rat in the bathroom. And I bet there are rattlesnakes in the toilet."

Her mother laughed.

"It's not funny, Mom."

"I'm not laughing at you, honey." Andie heard a muffled noise as if her mother had covered the phone with her hand. Then she heard her say, "I'll be off in a minute, Alfonso."

Andie rolled her eyes. Great. While she and her roommates were stuck in the middle of nowhere, her mother was living it up in Steamboat Springs.

As she waited for her mother to come back

31

on the line, Andie glanced around. She was calling from the McRaes' den. It was a large room with knotty-pine-paneled walls. Two sofas draped with Navajo blankets flanked the stone fireplace, and an elk head was mounted over the mantel.

"Mom!" Andie shouted into the receiver. "Are you listening to me?"

"You don't have to shout, dear. I've got to get off now. Alfonso and I have a reservation at the Chez Louis at seven."

"Did you hear a word I said?" Andie screeched. "I want to get out of here!"

"Now, Andie. When I planned this vacation you told me you wanted to ride. Well, White Horse Lodge was the only place open this time of the year that offered both riding and skiing. It *is* the middle of the winter, you know."

"Skiing? There's not even a lift," Andie shot back. "And it's a working ranch, which means we'll spend all our time mucking stalls and chopping wood."

Her mother sighed impatiently. "I'm sorry, honey, but it's too late to make new reservations. Steamboat Springs is packed. And with all the snow, who knows when I'll get out."

32

"Does that mean you won't be here tomorrow?"

"I'll call you, dear."

"Then good-bye!" Andie slammed down the receiver. Clenching her fists, she marched into the McRaes' dining room.

Bronc, Nathan, Jenny, Jina, Lauren, and Mary Beth were seated around a huge table dotted with dishes of food.

"What did your mom say?" Lauren asked.

"She said—" Andie was about to repeat the conversation when Cole walked rudely in front of her carrying a steaming bowl of mashed potatoes.

"Is everything all right?" Mrs. McRae asked. She was following behind Cole, a platter of chicken in her hands.

"No, not real—"

"Oooo. Fried chicken!" Mary Beth exclaimed. Mrs. McRae beamed as she set down the platter. She had brown hair pulled back by a barrette and an apron over her shirt and jeans.

Andie sat down and leaned over the table. "Let me tell you guys—"

"So you finally made it!" someone boomed.

Andie looked up. Dorothy Germaine had

come in from the kitchen. Another woman was behind her. They were both bundled in layers of sweaters, and their cheeks were bright pink from the cold.

"Dorothy!" Lauren squealed. She and Mary Beth jumped up from the table and threw their arms around the Foxhall Academy stable manager. Dorothy hugged them back, then plucked off her ski cap.

"It's about time you girls got here."

"Where were you?" Mary Beth asked.

"Cross country skiing with Marge." Dorothy introduced the other woman. Andie thought the two looked like short, fat snowmen. "It was a blast."

"Cross-country skiing!" Lauren clapped her hands excitedly. "I can't wait to go."

"But we're not going to stay—" Andie began.

"Let's eat!" Mr. McRae came in carrying a basket of rolls. He gestured for everybody to sit down. "My wife has fixed a delicious meal."

Andie could only stare in dismay at the heaping bowls of food in front of her. Her stomach was still in knots from the conversation with her mother. There was no way she'd be able to eat now.

"It looks yummy." Mary Beth smacked her lips as she scooped up two pieces of chicken.

"The meals have been heavenly," Dorothy said. "And wait until you girls ride. Yesterday Marge and I helped Cole and Bronc bring down some strays from the winter pasture."

"Wow," Jina said as she passed the Jell-O salad to Nathan. "Just like in the old days."

Andie stared at her roommates in disbelief. How could Lauren, Mary Beth, and Jina be so stupid? Skiing *up*hill and chasing cows wasn't exciting. It was *work*.

But as the conversation continued, Andie realized she was the only one who was miserable.

She groaned silently. She might as well face it. It wasn't her roommates who were stupid. It was *her* for believing that her mother had actually wanted to be with her this week.

*You should be used to this by now,* Andie told herself. But no matter how many times her mother let her down, it still hurt.

**5**

The huge bull snorted. Andie stared at his flaring nostrils and red-rimmed eyes. He had her cornered against the fence. There was no way out.

"Help!"

"I can't help you, dear," her mother said as she danced past with Alfonso, her chiffon skirt blowing in the wind.

Lauren galloped up on a pinto pony. "Hey, Andie. This is great! Ride with me!"

"I can't-t-t," Andie screeched as the bull lowered his head and pawed twice at the snow.

Mary Beth and Jina skied past. "Come join us!" they shouted, waving to Andie with their poles.

"I can't join you! Doesn't anybody see? I'm

about to be gored to"—Andie's voice rose to a shriek as the bull charged—"death!"

"Death!" Andie screamed so loud, it woke her up. It was pitch-black. Her nightshirt was soaked with sweat, and her heart was racing.

Where was she?

Then she remembered—the bull!

She bolted upright, banging her head. "Ouch!" Gingerly, she touched her forehead. Now she remembered where she really was— in the bottom bunk in a cabin at the White Horse Lodge.

With a moan, Andie fell back on her pillow. What a nightmare. Not the dream about the bull—the vacation. She'd spent weeks worrying about meeting her mother, now she wasn't even here. And worse, she'd bragged for days about downhill skiing, indoor pools, and cute guys. What must her roommates think?

"Andie? Are you all right?" Lauren leaned over the side of the top bunk, her braid falling across her shoulder.

"Yeah. I just clonked my head on the bottom of your bed."

Lauren giggled. "I bet you forgot where you were."

"I was trying to."

"Well, I think it's fun sleeping in a bunk-house."

Andie sighed. Lauren would think anything was fun.

"Is it cold in here?" Lauren asked. "My nose is freezing."

Andie felt her cheeks. They were icy, too. "Yeah it is. Uh-oh."

"Uh-oh what?"

"We forgot to put wood in the stove."

"Oops. Should we do it now?"

"Uh. I don't remember what Cole told us to do."

"That's because you were too busy arguing with him." Lauren giggled again.

"Was not. He's just one of those know-it-all guys. I can't stand that type."

"I thought he was nice." Andie heard the bedsprings squeak as Lauren flopped back.

"Andie?"

"Hmmm?"

"I think White Horse Lodge is great."

*You would,* Andie thought to herself.

"And I'm sorry your mom isn't here. I know you were looking forward to seeing her."

Tears sprang into Andie's eyes. She wanted

to thank Lauren for caring, but she didn't want her friend to hear the catch in her voice.

Lowering her hand over the side, Lauren rapped twice on the frame of the bed. "That means good night," she told Andie.

Gulping back a sob, Andie banged back. "Good night, Lauren."

Blueberry pancakes, bacon, scrambled eggs, sliced peaches. Mary Beth's mouth watered.

She looked around the breakfast table, wondering who they were waiting for. Andie sat across from her, idly twirling her spoon. Her cheeks were pale, and she had rings under her eyes as if she hadn't slept well.

Mary Beth couldn't understand why. The bunk beds were pillow soft. She'd been so tired, she'd fallen asleep as soon as they'd turned out the lights.

Sitting beside Andie, Dorothy and Marge discussed the day's itinerary. Mary Beth figured it had something to do with riding, since they both wore cowboy outfits in extra wide.

Nathan and Jina sat next to them, and Mr. McRae sat at the head of the table with Lauren on his right and Jenny on his left. They were talking about something called a quarter of a horse.

"Good morning," Mrs. McRae greeted them as she came out of the kitchen carrying a pitcher. Cole shuffled in behind her, holding a pot of coffee and yawning sleepily. He wasn't wearing his cowboy hat, and his blond hair fell softly on his shirt collar. Mary Beth saw him glance quickly at Andie before setting the pot before his father.

When everybody was seated, Mr. McRae announced, "Dig in."

Mary Beth grabbed the pancakes, glancing around the table again.

Now she knew who was missing. Patch and Bronc. She wondered where they could be. Then it dawned on her—maybe they were partners! Bronc knew where the cattle were pastured and Patch had the brains. It would be the perfect heist.

"So what would you girls like to do today?" Mrs. McRae asked.

Andie shrugged. She was pulling apart an oatmeal muffin. "What is there to do?"

"I told the McRaes you girls wanted to work with horses," Dorothy said.

"That's right. We love horses!" Lauren nod-

40

ded her head. "The McRaes raise quarter horses," she told Jina, Andie, and Mary Beth.

"The finest in Colorado," Mr. McRae said proudly. "During the winter months we work with our yearlings. If you want, Jenny will assign each of you a yearling."

"What's a yearling?" Mary Beth asked.

All eyes turned to her. She flushed pink when she realized she was the only one who didn't know.

"A yearling is a year-old colt or filly," Mrs. McRae explained. "Most of our babies are only about nine months old, but when the first of January comes around we officially call them yearlings."

"Working with a young horse sounds fun to me," Jina said.

Mary Beth brightened. "Me too." She could easily handle a little baby horse.

"I'd like to learn how to ride Western, too," Lauren said.

Mr. McRae nodded at Cole. "Cole's in charge of the ranch horses."

"I'm big enough to help," Nathan piped up. He turned to Jina. "You oughta ride Scooter. He's the fastest."

Mrs. McRae passed Mary Beth the bowl of

41

peaches. "Maybe this afternoon, Dorothy and Marge can teach you how to cross-country ski."

"Uh, are there huge slopes to go down?" Mary Beth asked worriedly.

Dorothy laughed. "Mostly you go up."

"Cross-country skiing is a lot different from downhill skiing," Dorothy explained. "You glide along trails through the woods."

"Oh. That sounds easy."

Cole chuckled as he stuffed half a muffin in his mouth. Mary Beth wondered what was so funny.

While they finished breakfast, Nathan told everyone about his pinto pony, Paintbrush. "He looks just like somebody spilled paint all over him."

Mary Beth smiled, then peered over at Jenny. Like Andie, the older girl had been quiet during breakfast, keeping her attention on her food. Mary Beth knew Andie was glum because she was upset about her mother. But what made Jenny look so sad?

Well, she wasn't going to worry too much about Jenny and Andie. Things were definitely looking up. No downhill skiing, gentle riding horses, baby yearlings, and *great* food. Plus, the McRaes were really nice. She was going to like White Horse Lodge.

"Ready to meet your yearlings?" Jenny asked when they'd finished eating.

Mary Beth slid her chair back and gloomily surveyed the mountain of dirty plates and cups on the table. "Shouldn't we help clean up?"

"Oh, no!" Mrs. McRae made shooing motions with her hand. "You ladies are guests. Cole and Nathan will help me clear the table."

"Great." Mary Beth grinned. She was *definitely* going to like this place!

"Wear warm gear," Jenny advised as they headed out the door. "I'll meet you in the barn in ten minutes."

"This is so much fun," Lauren said as the four roommates hurried to the bunkhouse.

Andie made a disgusted noise in her throat. "You three might think it's a blast, but I don't. By now I should be whizzing down the slopes in my new ski outfit."

"I never wanted to whiz down slopes," Mary Beth said.

"And I get lots of opportunities to downhill ski back East," Jina said. "Being on a working ranch is new and different."

Mary Beth opened the door to the

bunkhouse and went inside. They'd managed to get the stove going again, so the room was toasty warm. Rummaging through her suitcase, she found her gloves. "Maybe we can go into town one day and buy a Western hat," Lauren said as she pulled on her ski cap. "They're pretty cool."

"You mean we're near a town?" Andie widened her eyes in mock surprise. "I thought we'd have to take the buckboard to the trading post."

Mary Beth giggled. She was glad Andie was making jokes again.

"Last one to the barn is a grimy old cattle rustler," Lauren shouted over her shoulder as she raced out of the bunkhouse.

Mary Beth dashed after her. Halfway down the steps, she dropped a glove. When she stooped to retrieve it, Andie jumped over her. Laughing, Jina darted around her.

Mary Beth ran down the snowy path, trying to catch up. When she reached the barn, she stopped short. Eight shaggy horses were milling in the corral. Andie, Jina, and Lauren were leaning over the fence, scratching their withers and foreheads.

"Aren't they cute!" Lauren cooed. "I want

the chestnut with the star. She reminds me of Whisper."

"And look, there's a dapple-gray like Superstar!" Jina exclaimed.

"But where are the babies?" Mary Beth asked.

"These *are* the babies." Andie had straddled the fence and was ruffling the mane of a mahogany-colored animal with long gangly legs. "I want this one. He's the spitting image of Magic."

"But these aren't *babies*," Mary Beth said.

"Did everybody pick their favorite?" Jenny asked as she came out of the barn carrying a feed bucket and a handful of halters and leads.

As Jenny drew closer, the yearlings whickered excitedly. A brown one pinned its ears back. Snaking out its neck, it bit the gray next to it. The gray reared backward, slamming into a palomino. The palomino spun around and kicked the chestnut, who ran into two others.

Mary Beth watched, horrified. There *has* to be a mistake, she told herself. These horses were big and rowdy, and they had huge teeth and kicked!

Hugging her arms around her chest, she backed away from the corral. She had to come up with a reason why she couldn't work with a yearling. There was no way she was getting near one of those dangerous-looking creatures—ever!

6

"Get back, you ill-mannered brats," Jenny said affectionately. She opened the gate to the corral. Mary Beth gasped. Jenny was going in there with them! Were they going to crush her?

"Hey, Joker, I think Andie likes you," Jenny said as she slid the halter on the gangly bay. The other yearlings crowded around, nuzzling her jacket, hair, and pockets.

"This is Joker's Wild," Jenny told Andie. "He's a handful, but he's Cole's favorite, too."

"We should have guessed," Lauren teased.

After putting the halter on Joker, Andie led him from the corral. Jenny shooed the other yearlings from the gate. They moved away, stepping carefully around her.

Slowly, Mary Beth let out her breath. Okay, so Jenny hadn't gotten stomped. Still...She shivered, images of giant horse teeth flashing in her mind.

"And this is Too Pretty," Jenny said to Lauren as she caught the chestnut filly. "She's from really good cutting-horse stock."

"What's the gray's name?" Jina asked.

"Silver Sky," Jenny said. "Mr. McRae has high hopes for her in halter competition this spring."

"I can see why," Jina said as she led Sky from the corral. "She's gorgeous."

Jenny turned to Mary Beth. "Which one would you like?"

"Uh—um," Mary Beth stammered. She could feel her cheeks growing hot. "I don't—I really—I think I'll help Mrs. McRae with the dishes," she finally blurted.

Lauren laughed. "Mary Beth's afraid of horses."

"Not all horses." Mary Beth defended herself.

"All but her lesson horse, Dan," Andie explained. "And he's more like a giant dog."

Mary Beth flushed and looked down at the toes of her boots. What must Jenny think?

"Then I have the perfect lady for you." Turning, Jenny walked over to the remaining yearlings. Mary Beth stepped on the bottom board of the fence, trying to see what the older girl was doing. Hand outstretched, Jenny walked to the back corner of the corral where a tan-colored filly stood off by herself.

The yearling greeted her with pricked ears. Jenny slipped on the halter, then brought her up to the gate, chasing away the others as she went.

"This is Sweet Lena," she told Mary Beth. "She's so gentle she keeps away from the other ruffians. Even Nathan can work with her."

Mary Beth stepped down as Jenny led Lena through the gate.

Sweet Lena *did* look sweet. She had big brown eyes, a mop of black mane, and a gentle face.

Sweet Lena wasn't even that big. Mary Beth could even drape her arm over the filly's withers—*if* she wanted to.

"Hello, Lena," Mary Beth crooned, holding out her hand so the filly could smell her palm. "What color is she?"

Jenny handed her the lead. "Buckskin."

Hesitantly, Mary Beth took the rope. She was careful to stand by the filly's left shoulder, holding her right hand about six inches from the halter ring. In her left hand, she carried the folded slack. She tentatively turned Lena so she was lined up beside Jina and Sky.

"I'll show you where the stalls are," Jenny said as she led the way into the barn. "There's feed in all the buckets. Don't let them charge in. You be the boss."

*Be the boss*, Mary Beth repeated to herself. Lena docilely followed Sky into the barn. It had a center aisle with eight stalls on each side. Above the stalls was the hay storage, and skylights dotted the ceiling. The stalls were bedded with sawdust, and the concrete aisle was swept clean.

"This is cool!" Lauren said. "How long have you worked here, Jenny?"

"Since this summer. Here's Pretty's stall. Sky goes next to her, Joker beside her, and Lena's on the end."

"How did you learn so much about horses?" Mary Beth asked as she passed by the older girl.

Jenny shrugged. "I've been riding forever. Now, I'll hand each of you a currycomb, brush, and hoof pick. Keep your yearling on the lead at all times. Make them stand with a whoa and a firm tug if they don't respond."

As she turned into the stall, Mary Beth pulled gently on the rope. Lena slowed, then daintily stepped inside. Mary Beth brought her around to the feed bucket, and Lena stuck her head in to take a tiny bite.

Mary Beth ruffled Lena's springy mane. "Boy, if you were Dan, you would have engulfed the entire bucket by now."

"Hey, Jenny!" She heard Andie call from the stall next door. "What do I do if Joker nips?" Mary Beth blew out a relieved breath. She sure was glad she hadn't chosen Joker. Picking up the currycomb, she began to rub mud and manure from Lena's shaggy coat. Immediately, the filly stopped chewing and wiggled her upper lip with delight.

Mary Beth grinned happily. This was going to be fun!

"Your name is perfect for you, Sweet Lena," Mary Beth said, giving her a hug. "Because you are totally sweet!"

"Who wants to ride?" Cole asked after lunch. The girls were sitting on the floor of the den playing Go Fish with Nathan.

Andie didn't lift her eyes. Even though she was sick of playing Go Fish, she still didn't want Cole to think she was eager to go anywhere with him.

"I've gotta ride out to the back pasture and check the fence for breaks. Dad says I should ask if any of you girls want to come."

"I want to come," Lauren said.

"Me too," Jina chimed in.

Andie peered over at Mary Beth. She was pretending to study her cards.

"Well?" Cole directed his question to Andie.

Slowly, she shifted her gaze to him. He was dressed in a felt cowboy hat, jeans, chaps, and a heavy, all-weather coat.

*Pretending* to be a cowboy, Andie smirked to herself. He probably couldn't even ride.

"Do you really want us to come," she asked, "or do you always do what daddy says?"

Cole clenched his jaw. "Of course I don't want a bunch of so-called hotshot English riders coming. You'll just slow me down."

The smiles on Lauren's and Jina's faces faded. Andie cocked her head. "Good. Then we're definitely going with you. *All* of us. Right, Mary Beth?"

"Uh—sure, I guess," Mary Beth sputtered. "You do have a quiet horse, right?" she asked Cole.

"Right. In fact, I've got the *perfect* mounts for all of you." He grinned devilishly at Andie.

She crossed her arms. She'd grinned that way a million times herself. It always meant trouble.

Turning, Cole clomped from the den, calling, "I'll meet you girls in the barn in ten minutes. Nathan, you coming to help me bring the horses in?"

Nathan jumped up. "Yes, sirree, I am. Jina, will you ride next to me?"

"I'd love to ride next to you, Nathan."

"Yippeee!" He threw his cards in the air, then galloped off after Cole.

"Jina's got a boyfriend," Andie chanted when the two of them were out of sight.

"So does Andie-e-e," Jina sang right back.

"I do not." Andie slapped her cards on the rug. "Cole and I can't stand each other."

"Sure-e-e." Mary Beth, Lauren, and Jina bumped each other.

Andie jumped up. "Well, you three can think what you want. I don't even like Cole McRae. But I do know one thing. He's not going to call us 'so-called hotshot' riders ever again. We'll show him we know how to ride."

"But we don't know how to ride Western," Mary Beth pointed out.

Andie shot her a disgusted look. "Oh, come on, Finney. How hard can it be? There's even a big horn to hold on to."

Jina stood up next to Andie. "You still better listen to what Cole says, Andie. I'm sure their horses neck-rein and the signals may be totally different."

"Well, I can't wait to try." Lauren gathered the cards back into a deck, then scrambled to her feet. "It'll be just like the Wild West—cantering through the snow to check the fence line. Yippee!" she imitated Nathan.

Mary Beth winced. "I don't want it to be like the Wild West. I want a nice, civilized horse with good manners."

Andie grabbed her jacket from the back of the chair. She was ready to prove to Cole that she wasn't some dork from the East. She bet that devilish grin meant he was going to assign her the rankest horse they owned. But she wasn't worried. She doubted that any of their ranch horses were as green as Magic.

Ten minutes later, the girls had put on boots,

hats, long underwear, coats, and gloves. Nathan raced up to them as soon as they entered the barn.

"Jina! Jina!" Grabbing Jina's hand, he pulled her down the aisle. "I got you Scooter. He's fast and a pinto like Paintbrush."

Cole sauntered up carrying three lead lines. Andie hung back. He nodded to the first stall on his right.

"Mary Beth, you'll ride Sweet Lena's mom. She's just as quiet as Lena."

"Oh, thank you, thank you!" Mary Beth glanced in the stall and her face brightened. "She looks like her, too. What's her name?"

"We call her Mom." Cole handed her the lead. "Brush your horses down well," he told all of them. "They're shaggy and I just pulled them off muddy pasture."

*As if we've never brushed a horse before,* Andie fumed. Cole was treating them like babies.

"All the bridles and saddles are in the supply room under each horse's name," Cole continued, waving his hand at an open door on the left. "Just let me know if you need help tacking up."

"I'm sure we won't," Andie said.

Ignoring her, Cole headed down to the next stall. A blaze-faced chestnut hung his head over the half door.

"This is Mister Money," Cole said to Lauren. "He's my dad's ex-cutting horse. He's a little old, but a real good horse. I think you'll like him."

Lauren patted Money's neck. He snuffled her cheek, making her giggle. "I like him already."

"And, Andie, I brought in Rabbit for you to ride."

"Rabbit?" Andie arched one brow. "Oh, I get it. He hops around a lot, trying to buck you off, right?"

Cole stuck his thumbs in the pockets of his jacket. "Maybe." He grinned, then turning around, he strode down the aisle to the last stall.

Andie glared after him, simmering. *You're not going to get the best of me!* she thought. Taking a deep breath, she swung open the stall door. "Hey, Rabbit," she said, trying to keep her voice calm.

A dark-colored horse stood in the corner, his rear toward her.

"*Oh, great,*" Andie muttered. *Maybe he's*

*called Rabbit because he kicks like one.*

Reaching in her pocket, she pulled out an apple she'd saved from lunch. She took a noisy bite, then held it out, hoping he'd turn his head toward her.

"Ummm. How'd you like a taste?" she asked, smacking her lips.

Curious, Rabbit swiveled his head to look at her. Andie sucked in her breath, choking on the bite of apple. Now she knew why he was called Rabbit. He had the biggest ears in the world.

That jerk Cole had given her a mule to ride!

7

Spinning around, Andie flew out of the stall. "Cole McRae!" she shouted. "There is no way I'm going to ride a mule!"

A snort of laughter came from the end of the barn.

"It's not funny," Andie hollered.

Lauren stuck her head out from Mr. Money's stall. "A mule? Cool. Can I see him?"

Andie threw the lead down on the concrete aisle floor and slammed Rabbit's stall door shut. "You can ride him for all I care. I'm not going to."

Lauren's eyes widened. "Well, maybe it's just as well. You're in such a bad mood, you'd ruin the ride for everyone anyway." She ducked back into the stall.

Andie's face reddened. Suddenly, she realized how she must sound—exactly like some snobby Eastern rider. Just what she'd been trying *not* to do.

Slowly, she picked up the lead, opened the door, and went back into Rabbit's stall. She had no idea what to do with a mule, but she'd show that Cole—she'd figure it out.

"Okay, Rabbit." Squaring her shoulders, Andie strode past his hindquarters and snapped the lead onto the halter. Then she stepped back to look at him.

He had dark eyes ringed with tan, a slightly ewe neck, a black mane that stood straight up, and big hooves. Otherwise, Rabbit looked pretty much like a horse.

Cole leaned on the stall door. "How do you like your steed?" he asked, biting back a grin.

"Oh, he's cute," Andie replied, holding out the apple. Rabbit plucked it from her palm with soft lips. "All he needs is plastic surgery on his ears, and back East we could sell him for a Thoroughbred."

For a second, Cole didn't say anything. Then he tipped back his hat. "Hey, it was just a joke. Rabbit and his teammate, Jack, pull our hay sled when we feed. Don't worry, I brought in a horse for you."

Andie tried to look contrite. "No. That's okay. I'm sorry I complained. I'll ride Rabbit."

Cole frowned. "No, you won't. You'll ride Dakota. He's the bay gelding hanging his head over the stall door."

Andie peered down the aisle. Dakota bobbed his head. He had a star on his forehead, a cute dished face, and little ears.

"Well, okay," Andie agreed reluctantly. But when she unsnapped the lead line and swept past Cole, she grinned to herself.

She'd won this round. Well, maybe not *won*. But she'd proved to Mr. Show-off McRae that she could handle just about anything he could dish out.

"My toes are frozen, my butt is numb, and my nose is frostbitten," Mary Beth recited to herself as she trotted Mom up the snowy hill. "But I'm having a great time!"

She'd even tacked up Mom herself. Except for the saddle, of course. It weighed a ton, and she still couldn't figure out how Cole had knotted the girth. But the Western bridle had a snaffle bit just like she used on Dan. And since Mom was half the size of Dan, she'd been easier to groom.

Out of the corner of her eye, Mary Beth watched Cole, who rode a young sorrel filly named Crystal Sky. *Sorrel.* She was learning lots of new words, and just by imitating Cole, who sat straight and easy in the saddle, she was picking up this Western riding stuff.

Like the fact that just laying one rein against the side of Mom's neck made her turn. If she used leg, too, Mom *really* turned. Of course, Mary Beth had learned this the hard way after giving Mom a Dan-sized leg aid. Mom had leaped to the right so fast, Mary Beth would've fallen off if it hadn't been for that wonderful invention called a saddle horn. She had no idea why someone didn't put them on English saddles. It would make life so much easier for beginners.

Mary Beth shifted her weight, trying to ease her throbbing bottom. They'd been trotting for ages. And even though Mom had a smooth jog, Mary Beth wasn't used to so much bouncing in the saddle.

"Are we there yet?" Andie called from the end of the line.

Jina and Nathan, mounted on matching pintos, were right behind Mary Beth. Lauren and Andie brought up the rear.

"Why? Can't you handle the pace?" Cole asked without even turning around, though he slowed Crystal to a walk.

"This ranch *is* huge," Mary Beth said, coming up beside Cole. "How big is it?"

"About eight hundred acres."

"Wow. Is it all full of cows?"

"It's full of *cattle*," Cole corrected.

"What's the difference? Aren't cows the same as cattle?"

Cole chuckled. "Well, cows are female and give milk. Bulls are male, and the neutered bulls are called steer. Together, they're called cattle."

Mary Beth blushed. "I knew that. I think. So then why aren't you called a cattleboy instead of a cowboy?"

Cole gave her a funny look.

"But there are *cattle ranches*," Mary Beth babbled on. *And cattle rustlers,* she reminded herself.

"So how long has Bronc worked at White Horse?" Mary Beth said, changing the subject.

"Forever. Why?"

Mary Beth checked herself. There was no way she could tell Cole her theory about Patch

62

and Bronc being rustlers. He'd never believe someone who didn't even know a cow from a steer.

"On my way out here, I was reading about the history of the West," Mary Beth said. "Bronc looks like an authentic cowboy."

"He is. One of the last."

*Hmmmm.* Mary Beth pondered this bit of information. If Bronc was a true cowboy, then he knew everything about cattle.

"Where are Bronc and Mr. Delasandro this afternoon?" Mary Beth asked.

Cole shrugged. "Mr. Delasandro's one of those city slickers who wants to rough it when they come West. I think Dad sent them into the mountains to check the cattle pastured in the next valley."

*You mean to check on how many they could steal,* Mary Beth corrected.

Cole steered Crystal through a stand of aspens, and Mary Beth had to fall behind. After ten minutes of climbing, they halted their horses on a rocky bluff.

"This is White Horse Peak," he said proudly. Mary Beth rode Mom up beside Crystal. Her heart caught in her throat. Below them stretched a picture postcard vista of rolling hills and valleys. She hadn't realized they'd come so high.

"Why is everything named White Horse?" Jina asked. Her horse, Scooter, was small, but even after climbing for half an hour, the pinto chomped on his bit, ready to keep going.

"Some legend from my grandfather's time," Cole said. "You'd have to ask my mom about it. She remembers all that stuff."

Lauren's eyes widened. "Legend? Ooo. That sounds mysterious."

"Is the valley below part of the wild horse management area?" Jina asked.

Cole nodded. A cold wind was blowing across the peak, and he had to grab his cowboy hat. "In fact, sometimes we get wild horses straying onto our land."

"Do you think we'll see any?" Mary Beth asked hopefully.

"Let's hope not. None of the ranchers, including my dad, are crazy about wild horses on their property. They graze down the grass and tear up the water holes."

"But they're so beautiful!" Lauren protested.

"Have you ever seen a wild horse?"

"In pictures," she said sheepishly.

"Well, they're not always so beautiful. During winter or a drought they get boney thin, their coats grow dull, their manes get tangled, and their hooves chip."

"You don't kill them, do you?" Andie asked in horror.

"We don't kill them," Nathan piped up. "Do we, Cole?"

Without replying, Cole turned Crystal and headed back down toward the aspens. "Come on. Let's get this fence fixing over with."

An hour and a half later, they arrived back at the ranch. Mary Beth was so stiff, her knees buckled when she dismounted.

"This was worse than the foxhunt," Lauren said, rubbing her back.

Cole just grinned. "You'll get used to it. Cool your horses down, then leave them in the stalls. Nathan and I will give them some hay to eat until they're dry." When no one moved, he added, "Uh, you do know how to cool a horse, don't you?"

Mary Beth nodded wearily. Even Andie didn't have the energy to argue with Cole. After pounding fence staples and tightening wire, everybody was tired—*and hungry.*

*   *   *

"Do you think your mom would mind if I got a snack?" Mary Beth asked Cole fifteen minutes later. She was lugging her Western saddle into the tack room. The stirrups banged her shins, and it was so heavy she could barely lift it.

"My mom usually has an afternoon snack ready. Why don't you go on in and tell her we're starved?"

Mary Beth didn't need to be told twice. With a grunt, she heaved the saddle onto the rack and hobbled down the snowy path to the ranch house.

*Oooooo*, she winced. Everything ached. Now she knew why Bronc walked bowlegged.

"Mrs. McRae?" Mary Beth called when she entered the kitchen. A plate of muffins from breakfast was on the counter. Her mouth began to water.

Mary Beth reached for a muffin, then snapped her hand back. She better check and make sure they were for the afternoon snack.

Taking off her gloves and ski cap, she went into the den to find Mrs. McRae. There was a clunking noise coming from down the hall. The door leading into the McRaes' office was open.

"Mrs. McRae?" Mary Beth called as she walked down the hall and looked into the room. Jenny was sitting at the desk in front of an open file drawer. Her hand was poised above the files as if she'd been looking through them. When she saw Mary Beth, she slammed the drawer shut and jumped up.

"Hi! Were you looking for Mrs. McRae?" Mary Beth nodded.

"She went into town with Dorothy and Marge." With a guilty grin, Jenny darted past Mary Beth and out the office door. "But she left me instructions for a snack," she called over her shoulder as she fled toward the kitchen. "I'll get it ready. Dorothy and Marge also said to tell you that they want to show you how to cross-country ski when they get back. How's that sound?"

While Jenny rattled on and on from the other room, Mary Beth glanced into the office. Nothing seemed out of place. What had Jenny been doing? "Mary Beth? Are you coming?"

"Coming." As she walked back to the kitchen, she chewed her lip. Why was Jenny acting so strange?

Maybe Patch and Bronc weren't the only

ones up to something, Mary Beth decided. Maybe there were lots of mysteries at the White Horse Lodge.

8

When Mary Beth went into the kitchen, Jenny was setting muffins on plates.

"We sure had a great time with Cole," Mary Beth said, trying to sound as casual as possible. Taking off her coat, she hung it on the back of a chair. If she was going to find out what Jenny was up to, she couldn't make the older girl suspicious.

Jenny took several mugs from the cupboard. "I hope you got a chance to see White Horse Peak. The view's beautiful after a snow."

"We did," Mary Beth said as she washed her hands. "Can I help?"

"Thanks, but I'm almost done." She opened the refrigerator door and took out a gallon of milk.

"So, Jenny, what made you want to work at

White Horse Lodge?" Mary Beth hoped her question sounded friendly.

"Horses, of course." Jenny laughed and self-consciously brushed her bangs from her forehead.

"Are you from around here?" Mary Beth asked as she took a bite of her muffin.

"Well, I—" Jenny looked anxiously out the window. Mary Beth could hear Cole and Andie arguing as they came up the sidewalk.

Jenny made a leap for the door. "Here come the others. I'll see you later. I still have several yearlings to work with. Just call if you need me."

"Rats," Mary Beth muttered as Jenny escaped out the door. She was hoping Jenny would have at least told her where she was from. It was certainly an innocent question.

Mary Beth picked up her mug. The older girl was definitely hiding something. But what?

A tingle of excitement raced up her spine. Whatever it was, she, Mary Beth Finney, detective, was determined to find out.

"English riding *is* too harder than Western," Andie insisted as she threw open the door into the kitchen.

Cole stomped in after her, shaking his head. "No way. Have you ever tried barrel racing, team penning, or cutting competitions?

"Well, no. But have you ever jumped a four-foot fence or ridden in a foxhunt?" Andie stopped on the mat inside the door to take off her boots. Jina, Lauren, and Nathan crowded after her.

"Maybe I haven't foxhunted, but we've ridden after plenty of coyotes and jumped over rocks and brush," Cole said smugly. "That's tougher than dressing in a fancy red coat and following a bunch of dogs through the woods."

"It's a *scarlet* coat and they're called *hounds*." Angrily, Andie yanked off her wet boot. Why was Cole McRae being so stubborn? Even though her legs were a little stiff after today's ride, there was no way Western was harder than English.

Dropping her wet boot on the mat, she glared at Cole.

He glared right back.

Reaching down, Andie pulled off the other boot. It was on so tight, she had to hop on one foot while she tugged. "Argh!" Finally, the boot flew off. Losing her balance, she fell flat on her butt.

71

Cole burst out laughing and Nathan joined in. Even Mary Beth, Jina, and Lauren giggled.

Andie growled. "Ha-ha." Jumping up, she threw her boot down. "If you're such a smarty-pants, how'd you like to make a bet?"

"A bet? Sounds good to me."

Andie put her hands on her hips. "Good. Now let's see, what shall we win?"

"A movie," Cole said. "Whoever loses treats all of us to a movie."

"Hey, we like that idea," the others agreed. They were sitting at the table, hungrily grabbing muffins and mugs of milk.

"Then I'll take that bet," Andie said.

"Uh, Andie, don't you remember the last bet you made?" Mary Beth reminded her. "You know, the one where we ended up cleaning a bunch of stalls?"

Cole chuckled. "You mean she's always shooting off her big mouth and making bets she can't win?"

"Yes!" Jina, Mary Beth, and Lauren chorused.

"No." Andie shot them a nasty look. *Some friends they are.*

"To make it fair, let's let Nathan and your

friends decide what the contest should be," Cole said.

"That suits me fine." Dropping into an empty chair, Andie grabbed a muffin. She'd show Cole McRae who was the better rider.

Putting their heads together, Mary Beth, Lauren, Nathan, and Jina whispered excitedly.

"We've got a great idea," Lauren finally said. "Since both of you were bragging about your jumping, we'll set up a little course."

"Sounds good to me." Cole sat down across from Andie. Tipping his chair back on two legs, he tried to catch her eye.

Ignoring him, she took a bite of her muffin. "Don't pick jumping just to make it easy for me," she told her roommates between chews.

Jina, Mary Beth, and Lauren exchanged glances.

"Andie's right," Jina said. "Jumping might not be the fairest competition."

"How about a race?" Nathan suggested.

Andie's ears perked up. She remembered the race against Manchester School. She and Ranger had beaten all the slowpoke Manchester guys.

"A race sounds fair." Andie looked Cole straight in the eye.

Nathan grinned. "A race on Jack and Rabbit. The first one who can ride to the pasture fence and back wins."

*A mule race!* Andie almost choked on her muffin.

Cole sat forward, slamming the front chair legs on the floor. "No fair. Those two are so stubborn we won't get them out of the corral."

"You mean *you* won't get your mule out of the corral." Andie pointed her muffin at him.

Cole rolled his eyes. "All right. We'll race Jack and Rabbit. But I don't know how that's going to prove who's the better rider."

"Okay, we've set up the contest," Jina said. "When do you want to do it?"

"Tomorrow," Andie said, "first thing."

Cole stood up. "I'll be there." He grabbed a muffin and his hat, then strode to the door. "Don't forget, Andie, you can treat us to the movies tomorrow night." Shoving his hat on his head, he threw open the door and stomped out.

"You mean *you* can," Andie called after him. The door blew shut, and for a minute the kitchen was quiet.

"Gee, Andie, you sure are brave," Nathan finally said.

"You mean dumb." Mary Beth snickered. "There's no way you're going to beat Cole."

Andie bristled. "Of course I can beat Cole. I bet he's never ridden a horse like Ranger or Magic."

"But, Andie, have you ever ridden a mule?" Jina asked.

Andie shrugged. "No. But I bet Cole hasn't either."

"That's true." Nathan bobbed his head. "But he's ridden just about everything else. You oughta see all the stuff he's won."

"Won?" Andie repeated, her mouth going dry.

"Sure. Come on, I'll show you." Taking Andie's hand, Nathan pulled her from the chair and led her to the stairs. "He's got a whole room full of trophies."

"Hey, wait for us!" Lauren, Jina, and Mary Beth shouted as they ran after them.

Nathan led them to one of the upstairs bedrooms. The bed was made, but the floor was covered with boots, books, comics, and dirty clothes.

"See?" Nathan said, proudly pointing to the side wall.

Andie gulped. Shelf after shelf was filled

75

with ribbons, trophies, and prize belt buckles.

"Wow," Andie heard her roommates gasp behind her.

"Cole's won something in just about every kind of competition." Nathan hooked his thumbs in his belt loops and rocked back on his heels, imitating his big brother. "He even won a whole saddle."

"Well, a bunch of trophies doesn't mean anything." Andie stepped closer to read some of the inscriptions. LITTLE BRITCHES RODEO. 4-H HIGH POINT ACHIEVEMENT AWARD. GREAT RAPIDS QUARTER HORSE YOUTH CHAMPIONSHIP.

Andie started to sweat.

Nathan was right. His brother had won just about everything. And she'd only won a couple of stupid ribbons.

Andie wanted to kick herself. Once again, she'd let her big mouth get her into trouble. She might as well face it. There was no way she could beat Cole McRae.

**9**

"Well, Andie, looks like you better figure out what movie you're going to take us to tomorrow night," Jina said behind her.

Mary Beth giggled. "Or read a book on mule psychology."

Andie whirled to face her roommates. "Hey, whose side are you on, anyway?"

Mary Beth shrugged. "Actually, you're as stubborn as a mule. I think you can win this race."

"Or maybe Cole will break his leg before then," Lauren added with a laugh.

"Gee, thanks for the vote of confidence, guys." Turning, Andie left the room. She didn't need to look at any more trophies or hear any more jokes from her so-called friends.

"Maybe I can help you win," Nathan said.

He was tagging along on her heels as she rushed down the hall.

"Thanks. Anything would help." Andie took the steps in twos, stopping on the first floor landing.

"Ride Jack," Nathan told her. "He *loves* carrots. If you tie one on a string and dangle it in front of him, he'll chase after it and cross the finish line first!" He grinned proudly up at her.

Andie raised her dark brows. "Where'd you see that idea? In a cartoon?"

He giggled. "Yeah."

Andie squeezed him on the shoulder. "Well, thanks for the suggestion. At least you cared enough to give me one. I think my roommates have already decided I won't win."

She looked up the stairs. Mary Beth, Jina and Lauren were slowly walking down, talking excitedly about cross-country skiing with Dorothy.

Andie went into the den and slumped onto one of the sofas. She couldn't believe her roommates had given up on her so easily. Not that she blamed them. They were used to her shooting off her big mouth. And ever since they'd gotten here, she had been a jerk to be around.

*Only because I want to be in Steamboat Springs.* White Horse Lodge wasn't bad, but she'd rather be soaking in a hot tub or skiing down a pristine slope with her mom. *If* her mother wanted her.

Andie glanced at the phone. There hadn't even been a message from her mother all day.

A sob rose in her throat, and she burst into tears.

"When your weight is on the forward, gliding ski," Dorothy told Mary Beth, "kick down so the ski will grip the snow and propel you forward."

Mary Beth nodded, trying to follow the directions, but she had no idea what Dorothy was talking about.

They were standing at the bottom of the hill behind the bunkhouse. Mary Beth was perched precariously on two skis, her poles clutched in her gloved hands. Her feet were stuffed into boots that looked like running shoes with big soles. The toes of the soles were clamped to the skis. From the top of her boot to her knees, she wore nylon leggings called gaiters.

"Watch me," Dorothy said for the tenth

time. Mary Beth nodded again, but could hear the impatience in the older woman's voice. Marge had already skied off with Lauren, Andie, and Jina. Since all three had downhill skied before, they'd picked up cross-country skiing quickly.

Mary Beth just couldn't get the hang of it. Every time she moved, she fell. Now her gloves and jacket were soaked, and crusted ice hung from her sleeves.

Dorothy slid one ski forward, then the other, swinging her arms loosely and evenly. She glided up the gentle hill, then turned by flipping her skis up and around in the air, and glided back. She made it look so easy.

Mary Beth nodded. "Okay, okay, I think I've got it now."

Standing rigidly, Mary Beth inched one ski forward, then the other.

"Stop!" Dorothy held up her hand like a traffic cop, her pole dangling from her wrist. "I think I know what's wrong. You're shuffling. Hunch over like a gorilla, round your back, swing your arms, and stride ahead."

Mary Beth did as she was told, making hooting noises like a monkey. Dorothy started laughing.

Suddenly, Mary Beth's skis slid smoothly forward. First the left, then the right. She gasped. She could feel the rhythm all the way through her body. "I got it!" she shouted breathlessly.

But then she pushed off the front ski and it shot backward. Mary Beth fell sideways into the snow, her legs angled awkwardly underneath her. "Well, I did it—for a second or two."

Dorothy glided up to her. "Good! You felt the tempo. That's the important thing. From now on, it'll get easier."

"It couldn't get any harder." Mary Beth's ankles and knees ached. And getting up was the worst.

"Hey, guys!" someone shouted from the top of the slope. Lauren and Andie waved their poles. Both of them wore bright-colored ski outfits. The setting sun shone behind them like a halo.

Mary Beth shook her head in disgust. They looked like ads in a magazine.

Digging her poles in the snow, Mary Beth struggled to a standing position. "Isn't it dinner time, yet?" she asked Dorothy. But the older woman was skiing up the hill to meet the others.

Mary Beth pressed the tip of her pole hard onto the boot clamp. The clamp snapped open, freeing her boot. With a sigh of relief, she pulled her booted foot from the ski and set it on firm snow.

"How'd you do?" Jina asked as she swished down the hill and snowplowed to a stop beside her.

"Oh great," Mary Beth joked as she undid the other boot. "I only fell twenty-five times."

Jina laughed. "Sur-r-r-e."

"Well, maybe it was only ten times," Mary Beth admitted, but Jina had already turned to greet Lauren and Andie.

Picking up her skis and poles, Mary Beth limped back to the ranch house. The boots were pinching her toes and her ankle hurt. Between the afternoon ride and the evening ski session, it was a wonder she could walk at all.

"How'd the lesson go?" Mrs. McRae called into the mudroom a few minutes later.

"Stupendous," Mary Beth said as she bent over and unzipped the gaiters Cole had lent her. "The Winter Olympic Committee called already."

Mrs. McRae peered around the doorway. Smudges of flour dotted her cheeks. She held a steaming bowl of baked beans in both hands. Mary Beth almost swooned with hunger.

"That bad, huh?" Mrs. McRae smiled gently, then ducked out of sight. Mary Beth leaned against a wall to pull her nylon pants off. The door opened, and the others started crowding into the mudroom, chattering excitedly. Their poles and skis poked every which way.

"Ow!" A ski whacked Mary Beth on the head.

"Sorry." Lauren swung the ski the other way, knocking over a bucket of waxing supplies. Mary Beth burst into hysterical giggles. She hung up her pants, then hurried into the kitchen, to help bring in a bowl brimming with mixed fruit salad from the counter. She carried it carefully into the dining room, taking tiny steps, her eyes glued to the bowl so the juice wouldn't slosh.

She set it down and stepped back to admire all the food. Her brows shot up in surprise when she saw who was already at the table.

It was Bronc and Patch. Both had day-old

beards, matted hair, and bags under their eyes. At least Patch had a bag under the one eye Mary Beth could see.

As soon as they noticed Mary Beth, the two men stopped talking. But not before she overheard the words "cattle," "truck," and "sale."

Her heart skipped a beat. She couldn't believe it. They were brazenly planning the big cattle heist right at the McRaes' dinner table!

**10**

"Uh, hello, Bronc, Mr. Delasandro," Mary Beth stammered as she slid into an empty chair. *Play it cool, Mary Beth. This is your big chance to find out what they're plotting.* She racked her brains, trying to think of some subtle question that would expose the weaselly rustlers.

"Did you have a good time in the mountains?" she finally asked.

"Yup." Bronc pulled a grungy-looking handkerchief from his pocket and blew his nose.

Patch barely nodded as he sipped his mug of coffee.

Nathan bounced into the dining room. "Yay! Venison stew."

"Venison? What's that?" Lauren asked as she came in with Jina and Andie. Mrs. McRae

85

was right behind them carrying a huge soup tureen.

"Dee—" Nathan started to say, but a hearty "good evening!" cut off his words when Mr. McRae entered from the den. Cole, who had been feeding the horses, came in from the kitchen, his cheeks red from the cold.

Andie noisily pulled a chair out beside Mary Beth and plopped into it. "It *was* a good evening until Cole arrived," she hissed to Mary Beth.

*Oh, grow up,* Mary Beth wanted to tell her. Andie's rivalry with Cole was getting old. There were more important things to worry about—like Bronc, Patch, and *Jenny.*

Mary Beth scanned the faces at the table. Where was Jenny? The girl sure did keep to herself.

Marge and Dorothy sat down last. Mr. McRae was just about to say "dig in," when Jenny silently slipped into the chair beside him.

Mrs. McRae began passing the soup tureen. Mary Beth ladled out a plateful of the gravy- and vegetable-filled stew. Then she took two biscuits, spooned sweet potatoes and baked beans beside the stew, and dug in.

For a few minutes, everyone was quiet as they chewed and enjoyed the stew. Mary Beth surreptitiously eyed Bronc. He hunkered over his plate, shoveling heaping spoonfuls into his mouth as if he were starving to death.

"Mrs. McRae," Mr. Delasandro finally broke the silence. "This stew is delicious. Now I'm not saying Bronc can't cook. But that pork and noodles we gulped down last night just can't compare."

Mrs. McRae beamed. "Thank you, Mr. Delasandro. There's plenty of venison for seconds. But do save room for blueberry pie."

"What is venison?" Lauren repeated her question.

"Deer meat!" Nathan piped up.

*Deer meat!* Mary Beth froze in mid-chew. Jina's face turned white, Andie dropped her fork, and Lauren started to gag.

"Deer?" Jina croaked. "Like in Bambi?"

Nathan shook his head furiously. "Not like Bambi, silly. He was a cartoon. This is mule deer."

Mary Beth stared at the chunks of meat on her plate. Out of the corner of her eye, she saw Lauren spit her mouthful into a napkin. Jina politely swallowed hers in one gulp. After making an awful face, Andie pushed the meat to the side of her plate.

Mary Beth shrugged and started chewing again. What was the big deal about eating deer meat? They ate chickens and cows. Besides, it was fun trying new things. Like flying in a plane, skiing, breaking yearlings, and *spying*.

"I need to go into town after dinner," Mr. Delasandro told the McRaes. "Could someone drive me?"

Mary Beth's eyes widened with excitement. If Patch wasn't going to be around later, it would be the perfect time to snoop in his room. Maybe Lauren or Jina would help.

Tonight, she'd find out what Patch and Bronc were up to. Mary Beth smiled secretively. She couldn't wait.

"Pass the *Bambi* stew," Cole said. Leaning his elbows on the table, he directed his request to Andie.

Andie ignored him. It was bad enough having to sit near him. She didn't have to look at his ugly face, too.

Beside her, Mary Beth took the lid off the tureen and helped herself to more stew before passing it to Cole.

Andie wanted to puke. For someone who got sick just sitting in a plane, Mary Beth sure didn't have any trouble wolfing down deer meat.

"Elbows off the table, Cole," Mrs. McRae said.

He whipped his elbows off like some naughty little boy. Andie snuck a look at him. His blond hair was plastered on his forehead from his cowboy hat, and hay dust powdered his nose. Even his fingernails were grimy.

*Take a bath,* Andie wanted to tell him. But she didn't dare. She didn't want to give him the idea that she was even the teeniest bit interested in him. It was bad enough he was going to win the bet tomorrow.

Picking up her spoon, she pushed her baked beans around her plate. Just thinking about the race ruined her appetite. How would she ever get some stupid mule to do what she wanted?

"Andie? Would you like some more sweet potatoes?" Mrs. McRae asked.

Andie forced a polite smile. "No, thanks. I'm not really hungry."

*For this slop.* She'd be ravenous if she were

in Steamboat Springs eating lobster and filet mignon with her mother.

"Did my mother call while we were skiing?" Andie asked Mrs. McRae.

"No, I'm sorry, she didn't."

"Oh." Andie tried not to sound too disappointed.

"So, Mrs. McRae," Lauren said, her face still a little green from the deer meat, "Cole was telling us why the Lodge was named White Horse. He said it had something to do with a legend."

Mrs. McRae dabbed her mouth with a napkin. "Actually, it was named after a white quarter horse stallion my father owned. He bought the stallion from the King Ranch in Texas. He hoped to make the McRae Ranch just as famous as the King Ranch."

"The stallion's name was Wild Streak," Nathan said. "Isn't that a cool name?"

Jina smiled down at him. "Cool."

"But what's the legend?" Mary Beth asked.

Mrs. McRae picked up a bowl. "There's no legend. Lauren? More salad?"

"There is *too* a legend," Nathan insisted. Turning toward Jina, he wiggled excitedly in his chair. "Wild Streak was a killer!"

The conversation stopped dead around the table. All eyes turned to the little boy.

"A killer?" Andie asked.

Nathan nodded his head. "Yeah!"

"Now, Nathan," Mr. McRae said in a stern voice, "that's enough."

Nathan stuck out his lower lip. "But it's true! You said so. I heard you and Mom talking about it once."

Mrs. McRae's cheeks grew pink, and Mr. McRae's eyes narrowed. *What was going on?* Andie wondered.

"You'll have to excuse my son." Mr. McRae smiled apologetically at the guests. "He enjoys being the center of attention."

Nathan's lower lip began to quiver. "Do not. I heard you say that Wild Streak throwed Great-aunt Ellie. That's why she was crippled and died. That's why Wild Streak was called a killer."

*Wow, what a great story.* Andie glanced at Cole. He was hunched over his plate, eyes downcast, still eating.

*He knows the story's true, too*, Andie thought. Otherwise, he'd be poking fun at his little brother.

"Now, only some of that is true, Nathan,"

Mrs. McRae admitted. "But it wasn't Wild Streak's fault that Ellie got hurt."

Nathan grinned. "I know. It was my great-uncle Brett's fault!"

Just then, Jenny began choking.

"Are you all right?" Mrs. McRae pounded her on the back.

Jenny nodded, though she was doubled over coughing. Andie heard her take several ragged breaths.

"Grandma says that Great-uncle Brett was no good," Nathan declared loudly, trying to get everyone's attention back. "That's why Grandpa almost lost the ranch."

"That's enough, Nathan." Mr. McRae glared at his son. Nathan cowered under his father's gaze.

"I don't want to hear any more talk about Brett McRae."

"Why not?" Suddenly, Jenny jumped up. Her face was red from coughing, and her eyes glittered angrily. "Even if Brett McRae was responsible for Ellie's death, that was still no reason to drive him from his home! He loved this ranch. And he loved his family!"

All eyes turned to Jenny. Andie held her breath. She had no idea what Jenny was talking about, but she could tell from the stunned expression on the McRaes' faces that something big was about to happen.

"Jenny, how do you know about Brett?" Mrs. McRae asked.

Jenny pressed her lips together, and tears filled her eyes. "I know all about him because he was my grandfather!"

**11**

*Jenny's related to the McRaes?* Now Andie knew why Jenny had never answered any of her roommates' nosy questions.

Mrs. McRae dropped her fork. "Brett McRae was your grandfather?" She gasped.

Jenny nodded, her lower lip quivering. "Yes. My mother is his daughter."

"But why didn't you tell us?" Mr. McRae asked. He looked as shocked as his wife.

"Because I knew how much you hated him," Jenny said, tears spilling down her cheeks. "And after listening to you tonight—I know you still do!"

Pushing back her chair, Jenny ran from the room. No one moved. Mr. and Mrs. McRae stared at each other with horrified expressions.

"Wow." Nathan exhaled loudly. "Jenny's my sister?"

Cole kicked him under the table. "No, dummy. She's your cousin."

"That means she's *your* cousin, too!" Nathan tried to kick him back.

"Excuse me." Abruptly, Mrs. McRae stood up. Her face was as white as a ghost. Holding her napkin to her lips, she rushed from the room. Mr. McRae stood up hastily, his worried gaze following his wife.

"What's wrong with Mom?" Nathan asked.

"Finish your dinner, Nathan," Mr. McRae said, "then go upstairs and get ready for bed."

"Bed?" he squeaked, but when his father gave him a stern look, he quickly started eating.

"Cole, when you're done, check on the yearlings and bring in wood for the fire." Dropping his napkin, Mr. McRae excused himself, then left the table, too.

Everyone sat in stunned silence. Andie picked up her fork and speared a chunk of apple. She peeked across the table at Cole. He was staring after his father, a confused look on his face.

Not that she blamed him. She was pretty

puzzled, too. The whole conversation about killer horses, crippled aunts, and long-lost uncles had left her with a million questions. Still, it was obvious there was some deep, dark secret the family was hiding.

At the other end of the table, Dorothy and Marge began talking quietly to each other. Bronc, Mary Beth, and Mr. Delasandro helped themselves to more food as if nothing had happened. Lauren and Jina were glancing at each other with wide eyes. Andie could tell her two roommates were dying of curiosity, too.

"I wonder if that means there's no dessert?" Mary Beth asked.

Lauren and Jina burst into nervous giggles. Dorothy let out a guffaw, and even Mr. Delasandro cracked a smile.

Andie rolled her eyes. "Honestly, Finney, do you ever stop thinking about food?"

"Well, you heard Mrs. McRae mention blueberry pie," she defended herself.

"My favorite," Nathan mumbled, his mouth full.

"Only you're not getting any," Cole told him. He began piling empty plates in a stack. "Remember what Dad said? Up to bed. And you need a bath."

Slumping back in his chair, Nathan crossed his arms and pouted. "No fair. You guys will eat it all."

"Look, we won't have pie either," Cole said. "Okay?"

"Promise?"

He nodded. "And if you get ready for bed quickly, I'll read you a story."

Nathan brightened. "*Billy and Blaze?*"

Cole made a pained face. "Haven't we read that a million times?"

"Yeah, but I love it!" Shoving back his chair, Nathan ran upstairs.

After Nathan left, Cole glanced around the table. When he noticed Andie watching him, he dropped his gaze. Picking up a stack of plates, he hurried into the kitchen, awkwardly bumping into his father's chair.

Andie couldn't blame him for being embarrassed. His mom and dad had just made a major scene, and now he had to do the dishes, take care of his brother, and bring in a pile of wood.

She thought about the friends she'd hung out with over Christmas vacation. None of the guys would be caught dead doing all the chores Cole had to do. They were lazy and thought they were too cool.

Andie knew this would be a perfect time to tease Cole. But she didn't. There was something really wonderful about the way he helped his family. Something special in the way he and Nathan got along with each other.

A lump rose in Andie's throat. She didn't have a brother or sister, her father was rarely home, and her own mother hadn't even called.

Andie stood up so fast, her chair almost fell over. "Maybe we should help Cole with the dishes," she suggested to her roommates.

"That's a great idea." Lauren and Jina began gathering plates and silverware.

"I'll help, too," Mary Beth said, her cheeks bulging like a chipmunk. "Just don't take the salad. I'm not finished."

Grabbing two handfuls of glasses, Andie went into the kitchen. Cole's back was to her as he scraped food into the trash. She set the glasses on the counter beside him.

"Look, Cole," she said, "let's forget about the mule race."

He spun around. "Why? Are you chicken?"

Andie felt like he'd slapped her in the face. "Of course I'm not chicken," she snapped.

"Ha! Nathan told me he took you in my

room and showed you my trophies. The little worm." He was scrubbing a plate so hard, Andie thought he was going to break it in two. "Well, maybe a mule race was stupid. I think we should go back to that jumping idea. Just because I've got to wash dishes doesn't mean I can't lick some stuck-up smarty-pants rider like you at her own game."

*Stuck-up smarty-pants!* Andie's nostrils flared. How could she have even thought that Cole was a nice guy?

"I'll take that bet," Andie retorted, his sharp words ringing in her ears, "just to prove that you're wrong. You're the one who's the stuck-up know-it-all, Cole McRae—not me!"

"This is the craziest idea you've had yet," Lauren whispered to Mary Beth.

"You mean brilliant idea," Mary Beth corrected.

The two girls were sneaking down the hall to Mr. Delasandro's bedroom in the main house. Nathan was in bed. Cole was in the barn. Dorothy, Marge, Jina, and Andie were playing cards in the kitchen. Bronc had taken Mr. Delasandro to town.

Mary Beth wasn't sure where Mr. and Mrs.

McRae had disappeared to. But she knew this might be her only chance to check out Patch's room.

"What are we looking for?" Lauren asked in a hushed voice.

"Evidence." Mary Beth gestured for her to stop. The door to Mr. Delasandro's room was shut.

Slowly, she turned the knob, letting out her breath when it opened easily. "Good. It's not locked."

She slipped inside the room, waving for Lauren to follow. When she shut the door behind them, she let out a relieved sigh.

"Don't you think a cattle rustler would lock his door?" Lauren asked. The room was dark, and Mary Beth had trouble seeing Lauren in the dark.

"Not Patch. He's too cocky. He doesn't think anyone knows about him." She pulled out a small flashlight from her pocket. Luckily, her brother Benji was a Boy Scout.

Mary Beth shone the light around the room. There was a double bed, dresser, desk, rocking chair, and an open door that led into a private bathroom.

"Let's start over there." Tiptoeing across the

room, Mary Beth checked the bedside table first. She opened the top drawer. "Aha!"

"What?" Lauren peered over her shoulder.

Mary Beth held up a pair of eyeglasses. When she put them on, her eyesight instantly blurred. "That's evidence?" Lauren asked.

"Yes! Don't you see?" Mary Beth whipped off the glasses. "If Mr. Delasandro wears a patch over one eye, why would he need glasses with two corrective lenses?"

"Oh." Lauren didn't look convinced. She went over to check the top of the dresser. "What did you think about Jenny's announcement at dinner?"

Mary Beth tucked the glasses back in the drawer. "I was surprised, but this afternoon I caught her snooping in the McRaes' office. I knew something was up."

"Snooping in the office?" Lauren turned back to Mary Beth. "What do you think she was looking for?"

Mary Beth shrugged. "Maybe something about her grandfather. Hey, what's this?" She went over to a small rolltop desk. A notebook was lying open on the blotter. The top of the page was dated January 3.

"That's today's date. This must be a journal

of some kind." She aimed the light on the page. As she read to herself, her heart began to race.

"This is all about the trip Patch took with Bronc. He's written down the number of cattle they saw and where they're pastured." She tapped the page excitedly. "Lauren, this is it! It's the evidence we need!"

Suddenly, Mary Beth heard a door open and the sound of someone walking down the hall. The footsteps were coming closer.

Beside her, Lauren gasped.

"Quick, we've got to hide," Mary Beth hissed to her friend. "Somebody's coming!"

Mary Beth flicked off the flashlight. Grabbing Lauren's hand, she jerked her down to the floor. They wiggled under the bed just as the door swung open.

Light from the hall spilled into the room. Feet clumped across the rug, stopping about a foot from Mary Beth's nose. She held her breath.

Mary Beth stared at the person's shoes. Not only were they too small for Patch, but they were ladies-type Keds. Was it Jenny?

There was a soft thud above them, then the person turned and went out, shutting the door behind them.

"Whew. That was close," Lauren said, her breath tickling Mary Beth's ear. "I can't believe Mrs. McRae didn't catch us."

"Do you think it was Mrs. McRae?"

"Yeah. I recognized her Keds."

*What would Mrs. McRae be doing in Patch's room?* Mary Beth thought. *And what was that thud on the bed?*

"Doesn't that seem strange?" Mary Beth asked.

"No. It is her house." Lauren sneezed. "I've got to get out from under here."

After they crawled out, Mary Beth clicked on her flashlight again. A pile of newly washed and folded clothes lay on the bed.

Lauren smothered a giggle. "The Case of the Clean Clothes."

"Very funny."

"Come on." Lauren tugged on Mary Beth's sleeve. "Let's get out of here. Bronc and Patch may be back any minute."

"But we didn't get any evidence." Mary Beth glanced longingly at the journal still on the desk. She wished there was some way she could take it and copy the pages.

"Maybe not. But you've convinced me that there is definitely something weird going on. Together, we can keep an eye on Patch. Okay?"

"Okay. And maybe, just maybe, Mr. Delasandro—if that's his real name—will slip up." Turning off the flashlight, Mary Beth chuckled. "Then we'll nail him *and* Bronc."

But as she followed Lauren to the door, her smile faded. "Only we've got to hurry and catch them," she told her friend in a low voice, "before they steal the McRaes' cattle!"

"Gin!" Dorothy announced as she lay down her hand of cards.

Andie let out a disgusted snort. There was no way she was going to win a game. She just couldn't concentrate.

Leaning back in the kitchen chair, she checked the clock over the stove. Should she try and call her mom again? *No.* She and Alfonso would probably be getting ready for a night of cocktails and romance.

"Are you going to bed, Jina?" Andie asked.

"It's only eight o'clock," Jina said, stifling a yawn.

Dorothy's friend, Marge, laughed. "Skiing and riding can really make you tired."

Just then, Mary Beth and Lauren came into the kitchen. They had stupid grins on their faces as if they'd been up to something.

"What have you guys been doing?" Andie asked.

"Uh." The two glanced at each other with guilty expressions.

"Reading in the den," Mary Beth blurted.

"Taking a walk," Lauren said at the same time.

Andie rolled her eyes. "If you're going to lead a life of crime, at least get your stories straight." She stood up. "I'm going back to the bunkhouse. Anybody coming?"

Mary Beth yawned loudly. "Yeah, I'm ready for bed."

"Me too!" Lauren chimed in, stretching her arms with exaggerated motions.

Jina handed her cards to Dorothy. "I guess I better turn in, too."

"See you girls in the morning," Dorothy said. "Mr. McRae promised us a trip to the wild horse management area."

A few minutes later, the four gathered their jackets and headed out into the frosty night. When the ranch house door shut behind them, Andie halted on the porch. "All right, so where did you guys disappear to after dinner?" she asked Lauren and Mary Beth.

"Us?" Mary Beth feigned surprise. "What do you mean?"

"Come on, Finney. You have guilt written

all over your face."

"Maybe they stole the pie and ate it," Jina joked.

"We didn't steal the pie," Lauren said. "We snuck into Mr. Delasandro's room."

"You what!" Andie exclaimed.

"To look for evidence that Patch is a cattle rustler," Mary Beth explained as she started down the steps.

Andie followed after her. "Finney, you are so lame. And, Lauren, I can't believe you went along with her."

"Well, wait until you hear what we discovered," Mary Beth said, and she launched excitedly into something about glasses and notebooks.

Andie didn't even listen. She couldn't care less about Mary Beth's stupid obsession with cattle rustlers.

As she crossed the yard, she looked up at the stars. The night sky was clear, and a half moon peeked over the barn roof. Andie noticed the lights in the barn were on, though the door was closed.

She wondered what Cole was doing out there so late. Practicing jumping in the aisle?

It was a wild idea, but she wouldn't put it

past him. He was pretty desperate to win the bet. Too bad he wasn't going to. Not after he'd called her a stuck-up smarty-pants.

"So what do you think, Andie?" Lauren asked beside her.

"Hmmm?" Andie turned her attention back to her roommates. They'd stopped on the path that led to the bunkhouse.

"Do you think we should go and talk to Jenny?" Jina pointed to the light in the window at the bunkhouse.

Andie looked back and forth at the three of them. They were staring at her with eager, puppy-dog expressions.

"Honestly, you guys are so nosy. Jenny's problems are none of our business. She probably wants to be left alone."

Jina tilted her head. "Andie's got a point. Jenny hasn't gone out of her way to make friends."

"True." Lauren nodded. "But we could just go in and say hi. She might be feeling really down. After all, she can hardly talk to the McRaes about anything. And if she doesn't want us around, she can always tell us to buzz off."

"Let's vote," Mary Beth suggested. "Everybody that wants to say hi to Jenny, raise their hands."

Lauren and Mary Beth shot their arms into the air. Slowly, Jina raised hers. Andie reluctantly flapped her wrist, too.

Good. It's unanimous." Lauren lowered her arm. "Maybe we'll find out why she never told the McRaes she's related to them."

Jina put her hands on her hips. "I'm not going in there if you're going to interrogate her."

"Me either," Andie said.

"We won't. We *promise*," Lauren and Mary Beth said together.

The four girls started up the path to the bunkhouse, their boots crunching on the snow. Just as they reached the steps, Andie heard a whinny.

She stopped in her tracks. "What's that?"

"A horse, dummy," Mary Beth said.

"I know it's a horse, but the sound's coming from behind the bunkhouse." Andie's eyes widened, and she looked at her friends. "There aren't any pastures back there, right?"

"Right," Jina breathed.

Mary Beth snapped her fingers. "Cattle rustlers!" She took off around the side of the bunkhouse.

"Hey wait!" Andie called, running after her.

She caught up to Mary Beth, who had stopped behind the bunkhouse. She was staring up the hill they'd skied down earlier.

"See anything?" Andie asked.

"No."

Jina and Lauren dashed around the bunkhouse, skidding to a stop behind Andie. For a second, all Andie could hear was her friends' heavy breathing. Then the whinny came again—loud and clear—as if the horse was just over the hill.

"It must be up there!" Andie raced up the slope, skidding with every step. When she reached the top, her feet slipped out from under her, and she fell face first into the snow. Pushing herself to a kneeling position, she stared into the night.

In the distance, a white horse trotted at the edge of the woods, churning through the snow with powerful strides. His head was high, his neck arched. His tail and mane flew behind him.

Andie blinked snowflakes from her eyes.

The McRaes didn't have a white horse. She must be seeing things.

Mary Beth came puffing up behind her. Grabbing Andie's shoulder, she gasped loudly.

"I don't believe it!" she exclaimed. "It's the white horse Mrs. McRae was telling us about. It's Wild Streak!"

**13**

Andie craned her neck, trying to see across the glimmering snow. The horse had vanished. Had he ever been there?

"Wild Streak?" Sitting back on her heels, Andie shook the snow off her mittens. "No way, Finney. You heard Mrs. McRae. All that happened years ago."

Lauren and Jina struggled up the hill. "Thanks for waiting, guys," Lauren huffed. She was holding on to Jina's arm. Snow clung to the front of her jacket. "I fell, but luckily, *Jina* was nice enough to help me up."

Mary Beth spun around. Grabbing Jina's gloved hands, she jumped up and down in excitement. "You missed him! You missed him!"

"Missed who?"

"Wild Streak."

"Don't listen to her." Andie stood up and brushed off her knees. "There wasn't anything there. It was just the moon making strange shadows on the snow."

Mary Beth frowned. "That's not true, Andie. There was something out there and you know it."

Andie let out her breath. "Okay, Finney's right. There was something. But not Wild Streak. Maybe it was those cattle rustlers you've been dreaming about, Mary Beth," she joked.

"And I bet they left prints." Mary Beth waved excitedly toward the woods. "Let's hike out there and check it out."

Jina and Lauren looked in the direction she was pointing. At the base of the mountain, the aspens rose like tall skeletons. Above them was a line of darker pines.

"That's about a mile away," Jina said. "We'd freeze to death first."

"Then let's ride out there tomorrow," Mary Beth suggested. "Maybe Bronc and Patch didn't go to town. Maybe they're out there right now, rounding up the cattle."

"Get real, Finney," Andie scoffed. "This isn't the Wild West."

"No, but you heard Cole. He said there are still cattle rustlers."

Lauren clutched her arms against her chest. "I think checking for tracks is a good idea. But can we do it tomorrow? I'm soaked. And I still want to see Jenny."

"But it'll be too late!" Mary Beth protested.

"I'm getting cold, too," Jina admitted.

"All right." Reluctantly, Mary Beth followed Jina and Lauren down the hill. They held on to one another, squealing and giggling as they slid in the snow.

Andie turned and looked back at the woods. Mary Beth was right. *Something* had been out there. It couldn't have been Wild Streak the killer horse. It was probably an elk or cow or maybe even a coyote.

Andie shivered, remembering its arched neck and flowing mane and tail.

It *must* have been her imagination.

"Jenny?" Mary Beth knocked, then opened the bunkhouse door. Poking her head into the room, she smiled hesitantly. Jenny was sitting on the edge of her bed, reading a book. She wore sweatpants and a turtleneck, and her hair was damp as if it had just been washed.

Mary Beth glanced around. The older girl's room was slightly smaller than theirs, it had two single beds instead of bunks, and it was very neat. Where were all her dirty clothes and piles of junk?

Lauren nudged Mary Beth in the side. "Go on in," she whispered.

Mary Beth opened the door, and the four girls piled into the room. For a few moments, they stood awkwardly in the doorway.

"Can I help you?" Jenny asked as she slowly turned a page.

"We were just wondering if you—um—" Mary Beth gestured in the air with her wet mitten.

"Needed some company," Lauren finished.

Without looking up, Jenny flipped another page. "No. I don't think so."

Mary Beth turned to Lauren with raised brows, wondering what to do next.

"Let's get out of here," Andie hissed behind them.

Lauren came into the room. "Is that a photo album you're looking at?"

Jenny nodded. "I have some pictures of my

grandfather when he was a teenager. The ranch house is in the background. It looks just the same." She pointed to a photo on the other page. "And here's one of him with his brother, Jonathan, Mr. McRae's father. My grandfather must have left the ranch right after these were taken," she said sadly.

"But why?" Jina rushed over and sat on one side of Jenny. "Why did he leave? And why didn't your family have any contact with the McRaes?"

When Mary Beth saw Lauren getting settled on the other side of Jenny, she sauntered over. Twisting her head, she tried to see the photos. They were black and white, and showed two young guys wearing fringed chaps, ten-gallon hats, and goofy grins.

"That is the mystery," Jenny said. "When my grandfather, Brett McRae, was kicked off the ranch he came East, married my grandma, and raised a family. He never talked about his family out West, but my mom said he died thinking about the ranch."

"Wow," Mary Beth murmured. "What a sad story."

"When I graduated from high school my mom gave me this album," Jenny continued.

"It was the first time I'd even heard that I had relatives in Colorado. My mom knew that her father had left the ranch under a cloud of suspicion, but she didn't know why."

"So you came to find out why?" Lauren asked gently.

Jenny closed the album. "I was going to write the McRaes, but I was afraid they wouldn't even answer my letter. So I sent them an application for employment instead—not telling them who I was, of course. I've been riding since I was little, so working on a ranch seemed like a good idea. The McRaes hired me for the summer, which is their busy season, and I decided to stay. What a mistake."

"Maybe not," Mary Beth said hopefully. "Maybe it will be okay." She sat on the edge of the other bed. Andie had slumped into the chair by the woodstove. Sweat was beading on her forehead, and she studied her fingernails with a bored expression.

Tears filled Jenny's eyes. "I don't think so. You saw what happened at dinner tonight. Mr. McRae didn't even want Nathan to say my grandfather's name."

Lauren touched Jenny on the shoulder. "But you didn't give them a chance. I bet when

117

the shock wears off, Mr. and Mrs. McRae will be happy to have you in the family."

With a sigh, Jenny hugged the album to her chest. "Maybe. But even if they don't want me, I still need to find out why Grandfather was kicked off the ranch."

She brushed the tears from her eyes, then peered sideways at Mary Beth. "I was snooping through the McRaes' files when you caught me this afternoon. I know it was dumb, but I didn't know what else to do. I was hoping to find some record of my grandfather's life at the ranch. None of the McRaes would even talk about the past."

"Until tonight," Jina said.

Mary Beth loosened the scarf around her neck. "If Nathan's right, it has something to do with Wild Streak and the sister that got crippled." She thought about the white animal they'd seen trotting in the snow. She didn't care what Andie said. It had looked like a horse to her.

"Well, I think you should tell Mr. and Mrs. McRae what you told us," Lauren declared. "And show them this album, too. Maybe they're ready to forgive and forget. It was a long time ago."

Jenny held the album tight. "Maybe." Her voice sounded distant, and she gazed across the cabin with a faraway look in her eyes.

Mary Beth got the hint. "Gee. I sure am sleepy." Yawning noisily, she sprang off the bed.

Andie, Jina, and Lauren stood quickly, too. As they crowded out the door, they all started talking at the same time.

"Night, Jenny."

"I sure am pooped."

"See you in the morning."

"I hope I get to ride Mom again."

"Everything will be all right, Jenny. Don't worry."

When they reached their own room, the girls were pretty quiet. Taking off her wet boots, Mary Beth dropped them in front of the stove. Jina stooped to throw in some more wood. Andie headed for the bathroom.

"I'm beat." Without taking off her coat, Lauren fell backward into the armchair. "I think I'll fall asleep right here." She shut her eyes.

"This *was* one crazy day," Mary Beth admitted. Sitting on the floor, she pulled off her socks. "Full of mysteries. Do you think Jenny

119

will ever find out why the McRaes hate her grandfather?"

"Let's hope so." Jina closed the stove door, and stood up. Soot streaked her cheek. Arching one brow, she looked at Lauren, then Mary Beth. "But I sure hope you two 'detectives' don't help out. I can't believe you were snooping in Mr. Delasandro's room. How'd you like it if he came into our room?"

"I wouldn't care," Mary Beth said. "But, then again, I'm not a thief, so I don't have anything to hide."

She was about to throw her socks in the corner, when a movement outside the window caught her eye. Someone was staring into the bunkhouse.

Mary Beth started. The hair bristled on the back of her neck.

The inside light reflecting off the glass made it hard to see who it was. Suddenly, the person ducked out of sight, and Mary Beth glimpsed a flash of black where an eye should have been.

Her heart pounded furiously. Patch was spying on them!

**14**

"It's Patch!" Mary Beth screamed. Jumping up, she pointed a trembling finger at the window. "Outside! He's looking at us!"

Lauren ran over to Mary Beth and started screaming, too. Jina spun around to face the window.

The bathroom door flew open. Andie dashed out, a towel wrapped around her. "What's the matter?"

"It's Patch!" Mary Beth cried, running for the door. "I saw him!"

She threw open the door with Jina, Andie, and Lauren close at her side. Sticking her head out, Mary Beth glanced right, then left. There was no sign of Patch anywhere.

Keeping still, the four girls listened. A horse

snorted by the barn. An owl hooted in the distance.

Mary Beth stared into the moonlit night. Nothing moved. Where had he disappeared to?

"Are you sure someone was peeking in the window?" Jina whispered.

"Positive."

"Should we go out and check?" Lauren asked, her voice quivering.

Mary Beth wiggled her bare toes. "I don't have any shoes on."

"And I don't have any clothes on," Andie said.

Mary Beth peered over her shoulder at Lauren. She still wore her coat, hat and boots.

Lauren's eyes flew wide. "Uhn uhn. No way. Forget it."

"Maybe we should tell the McRaes," Jina suggested.

Andie laughed harshly. "Like they're going to believe us." She wrapped the towel tighter around her and went back into the room. "I'm not even sure I believe it. I think it's just Finney's overactive imagination. I mean, she's the one who claims Wild Streak was galloping behind the bunkhouse."

Mary Beth slammed the door shut, then stomped after Andie. "I do not have an overactive imagination. You saw that horse, too."

"Yeah. But I haven't seen rustlers in every plane seat and dark corner," Andie countered.

Jina went over to the window and pulled the curtains shut. "There. Now no one can see in."

"Do you think it's safe to go to bed?" Lauren asked shakily. She was still huddled by the door.

Andie shot Mary Beth an accusing look. "Now look what you've done, Finney. You've got Lauren scared to death." Striding across the floor, Andie gripped Lauren's shoulder with her free hand and gave her a shake. "There are no cattle rustlers at the ranch, Lauren. The only strange person is Mary Beth. And we know she's harmless."

Mary Beth sat there and fumed. "Okay. So don't believe me." She shook her finger at Andie. "But when the McRaes' cattle are stolen, you'll know I'm not making this up."

"Look, we're all tired," Jina said calmly. "Let's talk about this tomorrow. Then we can check for prints outside the window."

"Good idea." Mary Beth glared at Andie,

then marched over to the dresser. She yanked open a drawer and pulled out her flannel pajamas.

So what if her roommates didn't believe her? She didn't care. She knew that Patch had been peeking at them through the window.

Mary Beth was closing the drawer when a chill raced up her arms. What if he'd been spying on them because he knew she and Lauren had snooped around in his room?

Mary Beth swallowed hard. If Patch *was* a dangerous cattle rustler, and he knew they were on to him, then she and Lauren were in *big* trouble.

"Told you so." Andie pointed at the snow beneath the bunkhouse window. The girls were on their way to breakfast and had stopped to check for tracks. "Not one footprint. Unless Mr. Delasandro can fly, he couldn't have been spying in our window last night."

"But, but—" Mary Beth sputtered as she bent down to inspect the snow. "I saw him."

"Sur-r-e you did." Andie stepped out of the way so Lauren and Jina could see, too. "Just like you saw Wild Streak."

Andie knew she shouldn't be giving Mary

Beth such a hard time, but she was feeling lousy. Her head ached and her stomach was tied in knots. All because of this stupid jumping contest. Why had she bet Cole McRae that she was the better rider?

Now it seemed like a really dumb idea. If she hadn't been in such a bad mood about her mother, and Cole wasn't such a know-it-all, she never would have challenged him in the first place.

"I know what happened. Patch erased the prints!" Mary Beth announced triumphantly. "Look at the brush marks. It looks as if someone tried to smooth the snow with a glove."

"Right," Andie muttered, bored with Finney and her stupid Peeping Tom. Her mind was on the contest. She had to figure some way to get out of it.

An idea bounced into her head. Excited, Andie headed for the ranch house. She knew what to do. She'd go see her mom in Steamboat Springs. That would solve all her problems—she'd finally get to see her mom, and she'd get out of this stupid bet.

"Hey! Don't you want to see the brush marks?" Mary Beth called after her.

Andie shook her head as she bounded up

the ranch house steps. When she opened the door, the smell of homemade rolls greeted her. She rushed into the den, pulling her mother's phone number from her jacket pocket.

She dialed. It seemed to ring forever.

"Hello," a sleepy voice finally mumbled.

"Hi. Did I wake you?"

"Who's this?"

*What do you mean, who's this!* Andie fumed. "It's your daughter. Remember me?"

"Of course, sweetie. It's just so early. You woke me up." There was the sound of a huge yawn. "What's wrong?"

"Nothing. I decided that since you can't come here, I'd come see you. Today. This morning. The weather's gorgeous."

There was a long pause. Andie wrapped the cord around her wrist. The silence was making her nervous. Why didn't her mother say something?

"I don't think that's such a good idea, Andie," her mother finally said. "The roads outside of town still aren't clear, and Steamboat's expecting another storm."

"That's okay," Andie blurted. "The McRaes have a four-wheel-drive truck with big snow tires. They'll be able to get me there. And I bet they can bring you back here, too."

"That sounds great, Andie, but you don't understand," her mother continued. "The mountain roads between here and—"

Anger welled in Andie's chest. She couldn't believe her mother was saying no.

"Oh, but I *do* understand," Andie snapped, cutting off her mother's lame excuses. "I understand that you don't want to see me—ever!"

She slammed down the phone. Tears pricked her eyes.

A noise behind her made her whirl around. She spotted Cole hurrying down the hall. He must have come down the steps while she was talking...and heard everything.

Andie wanted to break down and cry. She wanted to throw the phone into the wall. Instead, she bit her lip—hard.

She didn't want anyone to know how upset she was about her mother—especially Cole McRae. It would be her miserable secret.

**15**

"Ready?" Lauren asked. She glanced expectantly at Andie and raised her arm.

Andie licked her dry lips. She was poised over Dakota's neck, the reins taut, ready to go. Cole and Mom had just cleared the hodgepodge of hurdles in record time. They'd had a perfect round until Mom slipped in the muddy snow and knocked down a broom handle crossbar. If Andie hadn't seen it with her own eyes, she never would have believed the old mare could jump that well.

But Dakota was younger and faster. Andie could feel his muscles bunch beneath her as he danced sideways eagerly. For this race, Andie had decided to ride bareback. She didn't want the horn poking her in the stomach or the heavy saddle slowing her down.

Andie took a deep breath, then looked at Lauren and nodded.

"Go!" Lauren yelled, dropping her arm.

Andie pressed her heels into Dakota's sides, and he charged forward, his hooves digging into the snow. Andie steered him toward the first fence—a two-by-four set on two over-turned buckets. Dakota hopped it awkwardly.

Andie clung to his mane with her left hand, as they landed. With her right, she turned him hard to the next obstacle—a stack of hay bales. She had to beat Mom's time with no faults.

Dakota popped the hay bales, eyeing them warily as he leaped. Andie could hear her roommates cheering. Even Nathan was yelling, "Go, go, go!"

Andie's heart raced with excitement as she reined Dakota toward the broom handles. He snorted, then slowed. Andie dug her heels into his sides and, sitting deep, urged him on with her voice and seat. He took off from five feet away, landing hard.

Andie stubbornly hung on. She had to win!

Turning left, she aimed Dakota at the last fence—two feed sacks draped over a pole. It was only about a foot high, but the edges of the sacks rippled in the wind as if they were alive.

As they approached the fence, Dakota tossed his head. His ears flicked and his muscles tensed.

"That's okay, that's okay," Andie soothed as she urged him forward with aching calves. Two strides from the sacks, she leaned forward and grabbed mane, ready for the final jump.

Unfortunately, Dakota wasn't. Ducking his head, Dakota slid to an abrupt stop.

Andie pitched forward. The mane ripped from her fingers as she flew over the horse's head and landed with a *plop* in the squishy snow.

Reins dragging, Dakota trotted off.

Andie rolled onto her back. Shouts of "Are you all right?" echoed across the paddock. Sitting up, she covered her face with her muddy hands, pressing her fingertips against her eyes to hold back the tears.

*Yes, I am all right*, she thought. *Nothing is broken. Nothing even hurts.*

*If you didn't count the pain of losing.*

Turning in her saddle, Mary Beth glanced back at Jenny. The older girl was riding a young colt, straggling behind the line of riders. Jenny's eyes were downcast, and she hadn't said a word the whole morning.

Mary Beth gave Lauren a worried look— the two were riding side by side. Lauren just shook her head sadly. Mary Beth wished there was something they could do.

Suddenly a branch whacked Mary Beth on the cheek. She spun back around. Mr. McRae had turned off the path that led to the wild horse management area. Now he was heading into a stand of spruce and lodgepole pines.

Behind Mr. McRae rode Dorothy, Marge, Cole, Nathan, Jina, Mr. Delasandro, and Andie. Mary Beth wasn't at all happy that Patch had come along. Just looking at him gave her the creeps.

Even though she couldn't prove it, she was sure Patch was planning something. They hadn't found any horse tracks by the woods behind the bunkhouse. And they hadn't found any footprints by the window. But that just showed that Patch was sneaky and smart.

When they came to a clearing, Mary Beth tugged on the reins, halting Mom. Lauren stopped, too. "Do you think Andie's okay?"

Lauren asked. "She's been awfully quiet since she got dumped."

"Just hurt pride," said Mary Beth. "I'm more concerned about Jenny."

Lauren nodded. "Me too."

"What's wrong?" Jenny asked as she rode up. Jenny's colt chewed on his bit and fidgeted sideways. Mary Beth didn't know his name. He was one of the two-year-olds that Jenny was training.

"We're worried about you," Lauren said. "Did you ever talk to the McRaes?"

Jenny shook her head. "No." Then she gave them a hard look. "Thanks for being concerned, but this is my problem. Okay?"

Without waiting for a reply, Jenny rode off, jogging the colt to catch up to the rest of the group.

"What do you think?" Mary Beth asked in a low voice.

"I think we'd better figure out a way to help her," Lauren replied.

Mary Beth nodded. "I agree. Somehow, we've got to get the McRaes to—"

A shrill whistle interrupted Mary Beth. Mom pricked up her ears.

"We'd better hurry," Lauren said, urging

Mr. Money into a trot. Mary Beth followed, posting as they wound through the pines. The rest of the group had stopped on top of a rise. Mary Beth noticed that Andie had halted Dakota as far from Cole as possible.

Mary Beth knew Andie was bent out of shape—there was no doubt in anyone's mind that Cole had won the bet.

"You need to keep up, girls," Mr. McRae said. "We've got trouble."

*Trouble?* Mary Beth peeked nervously at Patch. He was slumped in the saddle, his gloved hand resting on the horn, his eyes on Mr. McRae.

"We've lost some broodmares," Mr. McRae explained. Lifting up his hat, he smoothed his hair, then settled it back on his head. Beside him, Nathan did the same.

Mary Beth leaned over to Lauren. "What are broodmares?"

"They're horses that are in foal," Lauren whispered back.

"How can you lose one?"

"I don't know."

"Cole, you take Andie, Mr. Delasandro, Dorothy, Marge, and Jina and head over to the south side of the pasture," Mr. McRae instructed. "Lauren, Jenny, and Mary Beth, you come with me and Nathan. I'm sure the mares are somewhere close by. We'll need to find them."

Mary Beth gave Lauren the thumbs-up sign. Since Jenny was with them in Mr. McRae's group, they might have a chance to get the two to talk.

Cole rode off, the others trotting behind. Mary Beth breathed a sigh of relief when Patch disappeared from sight. At least she wouldn't have to worry about him knocking her off her horse and trampling her to death.

"We'll check the fence line first," Mr. McRae said, reining his horse to the left. "Maybe there's a break somewhere."

As they picked their way down a barren gully, Mary Beth steered Mom beside Mr. McRae. When she was sure that Jenny was within earshot, she said, "I sure would love to hear more about Wild Streak."

"Me too," Lauren chimed in. "What you told us last night was so interesting."

"Tell me too!" Nathan called. Clucking to Paintbrush, he trotted up beside his dad.

Mr. McRae looked suspiciously from Lauren to Mary Beth to Nathan. "You three don't have to gang up on me," he said.

"Yes, we do," Nathan declared. "I want Jenny to be my cousin! I like her!"

Jenny blushed bright red.

Mr. McRae sighed. "She's your second cousin, Nathan," he corrected.

Jenny looked sharply at Mr. McRae, as if she didn't quite believe what she'd heard. "Do you mean it?" she asked.

Without taking his eyes off the rocky path, he nodded.

Jenny looked down at her hands. "I'm sorry if I took you by surprise last night," she said. "I didn't mean to upset the family. I've wanted to tell you who I was ever since I arrived, but it never seemed like the right time."

"Maybe if we'd given you the right time, you wouldn't have had to surprise us," Mr. McRae said. "And I'm sorry we overreacted. It was an old hurt between Brett and my father. Now they're both dead. There's no longer any reason to keep past hurts alive."

"But what happened?" Jenny asked. "Why did my grandfather have to leave the ranch?" Mary Beth held her breath, hoping that Mr. McRae had the answers.

Mr. McRae shook his head. "I'm not sure. When Uncle Brett went east, I wasn't even born. And later, my parents wouldn't talk about it."

Jenny pressed her lips together. "Someone must know."

Mr. McRae reined his horse around to face her. "Why? Why do you need to dig it up?"

"Because the hurt needs to heal," Jenny insisted. Sitting tall in the saddle, she met Mr. McRae's gaze without blinking.

Finally, he tipped his hat back. "My mother might remember. She was married to Jonathan McRae for almost fifty years. If anyone knows about the past, it's her. Let me check with my wife. If she thinks it's okay, you can drive into town and talk to her. Fair?"

Jenny nodded. Spinning his horse on its haunches, Mr. McRae loped up the side of the gully. Mary Beth could hear Jenny exhale with relief. Lauren was wiping her red nose on her sleeve and snuffling. "Oh, I'm so happy for you."

"Does that mean I can call you Cousin Jenny?" Nathan asked.

Reaching over, Jenny cuffed him on the brim of his cowboy hat. "Sure. Why not?"

The four of them quickly caught up with Mr. McRae. He'd dismounted in front of a woven-wire fence. One of the wooden poles was smashed flat and the wire crumpled.

"Here's what happened to our mares," he said, peering into the scrubby woods beyond. "They got out. We'd better find them before tonight. I can't afford to lose even one mare and foal. They're the future of this ranch."

Mary Beth gasped, suddenly realizing what Bronc and Patch had been up to. They weren't after the McRaes' cattle after all!

Clapping a hand over her mouth, she stifled a cry. "Mr. McRae, I'm so sorry. It's my fault the mares are gone! It's Bronc and Patch. They've stolen your horses!"

**16**

All eyes turned to Mary Beth.

"What are you talking about?" Mr. McRae asked. "What does Bronc have to do with the mares getting out? And who is Patch?"

Mary Beth clutched the saddle horn. "Patch is Mr. Delasandro," she explained tearfully. "Only I thought they were going to steal your *cattle*. Not your horses."

"We found a journal in his room," Lauren added. "He was keeping track of how many cattle you owned and where they were pastured."

Mr. McRae walked around his horse to stand between Mary Beth's and Lauren's horses. Tilting back his hat, he peered up at them, his thick brows furrowed in a V.

"Let me get this straight," he said. "You

girls *snuck around* in one of our guests' rooms?"

Mary Beth gulped. "Only because we thought he and Bronc were cattle rustlers," she explained.

Suddenly, Nathan burst out laughing. Mr. McRae ducked his head, hiding a grin.

"Bronc a cattle rustler!" the little boy hooted.

"Not likely," Mr. McRae said, looking up with a smile. "Bronc's worked for our family for years. And Mr. Delasandro's from New York City. Not much call for a head of cattle there."

He chuckled, and Mary Beth turned crimson. Hastily, she wiped her tears with her jacket sleeve. How could she have been so wrong?

"Besides," Mr. McRae continued, "it was a four-legged thief that stole the mares." He jerked his thumb toward the crumpled wire. "The fence was knocked over by a horse."

"A wild horse broke down the fence?" Jenny asked.

"Yup." Hunkering down, he showed them several tracks in the snow. "My broodmares are unshod, but their hooves were just trimmed. The four-legged bandit that broke down the fence has uneven, chipped hooves."

"Yes!" Nathan hollered. "I bet it was Wild Streak."

Lauren and Mary Beth gave each other startled looks.

"Wild Streak died ages ago," Mr. McRae reminded his son patiently. "This thief must be one of the stallions roaming off the wild horse management area. Probably a young one trying to collect his own band of mares."

Lauren turned to Mary Beth. In a low voice she said, "Maybe it's the horse you and Andie saw last night."

Nathan pricked up his ears. "You saw a horse last night?"

"Uh," Mary Beth hesitated. She didn't want Mr. McRae to laugh at her again. "At least I thought I saw one—in the hills behind the bunkhouse."

"I doubt that was our thief," Mr. McRae said, straightening up. "No wild stallion's going to get that close to civilization."

"Then it was the ghost horse!" Nathan said gleefully.

"Ghost horse?" Lauren and Mary Beth echoed.

Mr. McRae sighed. "Nathan, there is no

ghost horse. That's just a story Bronc tells the guests to scare them."

"There is too a ghost horse," Nathan said, sticking out his lower lip. "I seen it when we went camping."

"You saw a coyote." Walking around his horse, Mr. McRae swung easily into the saddle. "Let's find Cole and the others and head back for lunch. Sorry we didn't get to see the wild horses, but I need to tell Bronc to fix the fence."

Mr. McRae's voice sounded worried. When he reined his horse around, Mary Beth could see the deep lines etched into his face. Suddenly, she forgot all about her embarrassment.

"We need to track down those mares," he told them solemnly, "before that rogue stallion hides them where we'll never find them, deep in some isolated valley!"

*Just say it, Cole.* Andie glowered silently at Cole's back as they rode down the hill. *Turn around and gloat. Boast that you're the better rider.*

But he didn't turn around. He didn't say anything about winning the bet. But Andie knew what he was thinking. He was glad the snotty Easterner had fallen on her butt.

It was after lunch. Family, guests, and ranch hands had saddled up and headed into the foothills to hunt for the missing mares.

Andie knew how upset Mr. McRae was, so when he'd assigned her to Cole's group along with Nathan and Mary Beth, she'd kept her big mouth shut. Now she wished she'd said something. It was going to be a long ride.

"See any more tracks?" Nathan called up to his brother.

Cole shook his head. "Nope," he called back. "The wind's drifted the snow." He pulled his collar higher up his neck.

Cole was riding the filly Crystal Sky. She picked her way carefully around the rocks and sagebrush that dotted the steep hill.

Andie shivered and yanked her cap over her ears. A cold north wind had picked up, blowing icy showers of snow off the pine limbs. Dakota's mane was frosted white, and Andie's cheeks were numb.

As they ambled along, Andie thought about her mother. She and Alfonso were probably snuggling in front of a cozy fire, sipping tea.

*It's not fair*, Andie thought. Slumping in the saddle, she plucked dejectedly at Dakota's frozen mane. Why hadn't anything gone right for her this vacation?

"So what movie are you treating us to tonight?" Nathan asked, cutting into Andie's thoughts.

Behind him, Mary Beth giggled. Andie rolled her eyes, then sighed. She had lost the bet fair and square, so she might as well be a good sport.

"You choose, Nathan," Andie said.

"*Raiders Revenge!*" Nathan cried gleefully.

Cole twisted around to look at his brother. "Come on, Nathan. You know it's rated PG-13. Mom won't let you see it."

"You either." Nathan put one fist on his hip. "You're not thirteen."

Cole swung back around in the saddle, but not before Andie saw him redden. At the bottom of the hill, he halted Crystal by a stream.

"Well, I give up," he said grumpily. "That stallion must have vanished with those mares."

"That's because he's the ghost horse," Nathan said.

Mary Beth steered Mom between Cole and his brother. "Is there really a ghost horse?"

Cole shrugged. "Bronc claims there is. He

says it's the spirit of Wild Streak. But I've never seen it."

"What exactly happened to Wild Streak?" Mary Beth asked.

"Mustang rustlers got him," Cole said.

"Mustang rustlers!" Andie exclaimed.

Cole nodded but didn't look at her. "It wasn't that long ago that mustangs weren't protected," he said. "Anyone could round them up and sell them for dog food or shoot them for sport. When Wild Streak ran off, rustlers shot him."

"That's horrible!" Mary Beth said. "Especially since he was your grandfather's prize stallion!"

Cole looked up at the sky and frowned. "Clouds are coming in. Our mares are used to food and shelter. They won't last long if a storm rolls over the mountain."

"We've got to find them, Cole," Nathan pleaded. "Jade and Lily are out there. They're my favorites."

"We'll find them." Reaching over, Cole playfully pulled Nathan's hat brim over his eyes. His little brother smiled.

Andie chewed her lower lip. She needed to quit worrying about herself. The missing mares meant real trouble for the McRaes.

"We'd better get back." Cole swung Crystal around. When he rode past Andie, he stole a quick look at her. Andie brushed the snow off Dakota's rump, pretending not to notice.

They headed downstream. Andie hunkered into her coat. Her toes were frozen, and her lips were chapped. She couldn't wait to get back to the ranch and have some of Mrs. McRae's homemade hot chocolate. And maybe her mom had called to say she wanted Andie to come after all.

Dakota broke into a jog as if he were thinking about his warm stall. In front, Crystal switched her tail and tossed her head, also eager to get home. Only Mom and Paintbrush plodded along quietly.

The group passed a thick grove of aspens and cottonwoods growing along the bank. Andie kept her eyes peeled, hoping to see signs of the missing mares.

Suddenly, an elk exploded from the grove. Dakota threw up his head in surprise, while Crystal spun around in a circle. Cole kept a tight seat, but when the elk bounded past, the frightened filly leaped sideways.

"Easy," Cole soothed, squeezing her with

his outside leg. But Crystal had shied too close to the stream. The snow-covered bank gave way under her rear legs, and her haunches dropped over the edge. The filly scrabbled frantically at the muddy bank, but unable to find a footing, she tipped over backward.

Horse and rider toppled into the stream. Andie screamed as Crystal fell heavily onto Cole. She was going to crush him!

**17**

The horse landed on her side, pinning Cole's left leg. She heaved herself up on her forelegs, then fell back again.

Andie jumped off Dakota, dropping her reins, and bounded down the bank. She waded into the stream and grasped the cheekpiece of Crystal's halter, which the horse wore underneath her bridle.

"Get up, Crystal! Come on, girl!" Frantically, Andie clucked and tugged.

Cole grabbed on to a root sticking out of the stream bank and pulled himself free.

"You can do it, girl!" Andie took the reins and smacked Crystal lightly on the neck. The filly lurched to her feet. After shaking herself like a dog, she clambered up the bank and greeted her stablemates with anxious whiffles.

Andie sloshed across the stream, ice-cold water swirling into her boots. Cole was lying on his side in several inches of water.

"Is your leg okay? Can you walk?" Andie asked anxiously.

Cole nodded, grinning feebly. As Andie helped him to his feet, Nathan slid down the bank and retrieved Cole's hat, which had gotten stuck on a rock. When he came up to his brother, his eyes were brimming with tears.

"Are you okay, Cole?" he asked, a sob catching in his throat.

Cole punched him playfully on the shoulder. "Sure," he said, but his face was as white as a sheet. Andie could see he was trembling with cold.

Together, Andie and Nathan boosted Cole up the bank. He held on to Dakota's stirrup until he caught his breath. Andie noticed he wasn't putting any weight on his left leg.

"I don't think it's busted," he said, gritting his teeth, "but my knee hurts like crazy."

"Somebody better take Crystal," Mary Beth cut in. She had dismounted and was gingerly holding the filly. "She's acting crazy."

Andie took the mare's rein. Crystal was staring off in the direction the elk had gone.

Her nostrils were flared, her eyes showed white, and every one of her muscles was quivering. Andie made her walk forward, then quickly ran a hand down each leg. Except for being wet and overexcited, she seemed okay.

"I'd better ride Crystal home," Andie told Cole. "You take Dakota." The bay stood patiently ground-tied.

Cole glanced sharply at Andie. "Crystal's pretty wound up. Are you sure you can—?" He stopped in mid-sentence and he shook his head. "Never mind."

Placing his left hand on the saddle horn, he slowly mounted, his jaw clenched in pain. Andie touched the hem of his jeans. The material had frozen stiff.

"Here." Before Cole could protest, Andie took off her coat and threw it up to him.

"No way. You need—"

Andie ignored him. Gathering the reins, she stuck her left toe in the stirrup. Crystal danced off, and Andie had to hold on to the saddle horn to swing herself up.

"Hey, Andie!" Cole called.

"What?" Andie straightened in the saddle. To her surprise, her heart was pounding. She must not have realized how scared she'd been when Cole landed in the stream.

He gave her a lopsided grin that made her heart beat even faster. "Thanks for the coat."

"Ellie McRae was as hardheaded as her two brothers, Brett and Jonathan," Grandmother McRae told Jenny, Jina, and Mary Beth that night.

The three girls were perched on the edge of a straight-backed sofa covered with lace doilies. Grandmother McRae sat across from them in a wooden rocker, a crocheted afghan on her lap.

Mary Beth figured the rocker and Grandmother McRae had to be at least a hundred. The elderly woman had pure-white hair smoothed back into a bun. Her crinkly skin looked like tissue paper, and she was so tiny, her body practically disappeared in the folds of her flowered dress. But her voice was clear and she'd seemed delighted to meet Jenny.

"I met Ellie after she'd had her fall," Grandmother McRae went on. "By then, Brett McRae was gone, but not forgotten. My husband, Jonathan, never spoke about him, but it was as if Brett's ghost, and the ghost of Wild Streak, haunted the ranch."

Mary Beth leaned forward excitedly. That was the second time today someone had mentioned the ghost horse.

"Didn't Ellie ever tell you what happened?" Jenny asked.

Grandmother McRae shook her head. "No." She gestured to a plate of homemade cookies. "Do eat up, girls. I make these for my bridge club ladies, but we always have lots left over."

Mary Beth took her fourth cookie. They were delicious but dry. Grandmother McRae hadn't offered them anything to drink, and the apartment was hot and stuffy. She almost wished she'd gone out with her friends. Nathan, Cole, Andie and Lauren were looking at cowboy hats and she'd meet them later at the movie theater.

Settling back in her chair, Grandmother McRae began to rock. Her black lace-up shoes rose off the floor each time the chair tipped back.

"Ellie kept her emotions bottled up inside," she said. "I think that's one reason why she died not too long after her fall. Of course, not being able to ride killed her, too. She loved horses. And then when Brett went away without a word, she seemed to shrivel up." Her voice faded.

Mary Beth glanced at Jina, who was nibbling at a cookie. Jenny was biting a fingernail and frowning. Mary Beth knew she was probably disappointed that Grandmother McRae hadn't been able to answer her questions.

"These cookies sure are delicious!" Mary Beth said loudly.

Grandmother McRae's lashes fluttered open. "Help yourself to another one, dear."

"Mrs. McRae." Jenny leaned forward. "Is there *anything* you can tell me that would help explain why my grandfather had to leave the ranch?"

For a long moment, Grandmother McRae stared at her gnarled hands. Then she suddenly looked up, a gleam in her eyes. "Ellie's journal! That might answer your questions."

"A journal!" Jenny almost fell off the sofa, and Mary Beth stopped chewing.

"Yes." Grandmother McRae frowned. "But I have no idea where it is."

"Would your son know or maybe Mrs. McRae?" Jenny asked eagerly.

"I'm afraid I don't know." Grandmother McRae's voice began to quiver.

"I think she's getting tired," Jina whispered. Jenny nodded and stood up. "Well, thank you for everything, Mrs. McRae. And I'm glad to meet another relative."

Crossing the rug, she kissed the elderly woman on her forehead.

"I'm glad to meet you too, dear," Grandmother McRae said. "You must come see me again. It doesn't matter that we're not really blood relatives."

Jenny smiled. "That's true. You married into the McRae family."

"No. I mean, in a way, you're not really related to us. You see, Brett McRae wasn't blood kin," Grandmother McRae explained. "He was adopted."

Mary Beth sucked in her breath and glanced at Jenny. All the blood had drained from the other girl's face.

"I see," Jenny said, picking up her coat. "Thank you for telling me." Hastily, Mary Beth and Jina retrieved their jackets, too.

After saying good-bye to Grandmother McRae, the three girls filed into the hall of the apartment house. Silently, they went down the stairs and stepped into the cold night air. As they climbed into the pickup, Mary Beth looked worriedly at Jenny. The older girl's mouth was drawn tight.

"Are you okay?" Jina asked finally. "That was kind of a bombshell, wasn't it?"

Jenny shrugged as she slammed the gearshift into reverse. The truck roared backward into the parking lot, narrowly missing a car. Mary Beth grabbed on to the door handle to keep from falling into Jina.

"Oh, it was a bombshell, all right," Jenny retorted. "What I want to know is, why didn't Mr. and Mrs. McRae say anything?"

"Maybe they didn't know," Mary Beth offered.

Jenny snorted. "Well, at least now I know another reason why the family didn't care enough to ever contact my dad or mom or me."

"But adopted kids are family, too," Jina said.

Jenny careened around a corner, and Mary Beth clawed at the window ledge. "Where are you going?" Storefronts and streetlights were flashing past. The town was bigger than she'd expected, and she had no idea where they were.

"I'm dropping you two off at the movies,"

Jenny said. "Then I'm heading to the newspaper office. I have a friend who works there."

"A boyfriend?" Mary Beth teased, trying to lighten things up.

Jenny shot her an annoyed look. "No. A friend who will let me look at all their back issues. They must have them on disk or microfiche or something."

"What do you want to find out?" Jina asked.

"If Ellie was crippled in an accident, then there must have been some kind of newspaper account."

"Oh-h-h." Mary Beth nodded knowingly. Now why hadn't she, the great detective, thought about doing that?

Whipping behind a parked car, Jenny braked in front of the movie theater. The old-fashioned marquee announced, DISNEY CLASSIC: CINDERELLA.

"I'll pick you guys up at nine, okay?"

Mary Beth opened the truck door so fast she almost toppled out. Jina jumped out after her. With a quick good-bye, Jenny zoomed off.

"Whew! She sure was in a hurry," Jina said.

"Do you think she'll find what she's looking for?"

Jina shrugged. "I doubt it. It was a long

time ago." She turned and headed toward the ticket booth. "I wonder if the others are here yet."

Mary Beth followed her friend up the sidewalk. Several other people were walking into the theater or hanging around outside, but she didn't see their roommates.

Suddenly, Mary Beth stopped in the middle of the sidewalk. "Hey, I think I know how we can help Jenny!"

"Uh-oh. I thought you were going to stay out of this. Lauren said you already got yelled at for snooping in Mr. Delasandro's room."

"I wasn't snooping. Besides, this is different."

With a sigh, Jina zipped up her jacket against the cold. "All right. How can we help Jenny?"

"By finding that journal!" Mary Beth said excitedly.

Jina looked doubtful. "Come on, Mary Beth. It could be anywhere."

"I know. But don't you see? It's the missing piece. It might answer all Jenny's questions. And it could even bring the family back together."

Just then, Andie, Nathan, Cole, and Lauren came up the sidewalk. The girls were wearing brand-new cowboy hats. Cole was on crutches, but he was making pretty good time.

"So, what do you think about the diary?" Mary Beth pressed.

"Does this mean you've given up on the big cattle rustlers?" Jina joked.

Mary Beth frowned gloomily at her feet. At dinner, Nathan had told the whole table how she had thought Bronc and Patch were cattle rustlers. He'd teased her about being a "dude from the East" and everyone had laughed.

"Yeah, I've forgotten about the cattle rustlers." Scraping the toe of her sneaker along the sidewalk, Mary Beth nudged up a wad of gum.

"I'm just teasing you." Jina punched her on the arm. "I think it's a real long shot, and we only have a few more days of vacation left, but I'll help you look for Ellie's journal."

"Really?" Mary Beth squealed. She punted the gum into the gutter.

"On one condition: We don't snoop in anyone's room without permission."

Mary Beth nodded. "Deal."

As Jina went to greet the others, Mary Beth tapped her lip thoughtfully. Finding the journal wouldn't be easy. But Mary Beth knew she had to try. She had to prove to everybody she wasn't some dumb dude. Before she left White Horse Lodge, she would solve Jenny's mystery.

18

"I've never heard my parents talk about any journal," Cole told Mary Beth as they waited in the theater lobby for Lauren and Andie to come out of the rest room. "And they never even mention Great-aunt Ellie. Kind of like they never mention Brett or Wild Streak."

"I've heard about Ellie!" Nathan announced. "Bronc told me stories about her."

Mary Beth spun around. "He did?"

Nathan nodded. "Yeah. Bronc was real young back then. But before Great-aunt Ellie died, he used to take her up to the mountains in the wagon. She couldn't walk, you know."

Jina leaned down so she was at eye level with Nathan. "What else did Bronc tell you? Did he tell you where he took Ellie?"

"To one of the line camps, I think. She'd

stay up there a couple days, reading and painting."

"Line camps?" Puzzled, Mary Beth looked at Cole.

He shrugged. "They were mountain cabins used by the cowboys who were hired to stay with the herds all summer," Cole explained. "We don't use them anymore."

"That's it, then!" Mary Beth bounced on her toes. "I bet Ellie kept the journal in the cabin! We have a break in the case!"

Cole leaned heavily on one crutch. "Case?" he repeated doubtfully.

Mary Beth nodded. "I'm going to help Jenny figure out why her grandfather had to leave the ranch. Finding that journal is important, and thanks to Nathan here, we have a clue about where Ellie might have left it." Grabbing Nathan, Mary Beth gave him a hug.

"Yech." Nathan pulled away, and the others laughed.

Mary Beth was so excited, she was about to burst. Wait until she told Jenny!

"You can be my helper, Nathan." Mary Beth gave the small boy a big smile. "And tomorrow you have your first job—helping Jina and me find that line camp. Then we're going to find that journal and solve Jenny's mystery!"

"I can't believe we're seeing a little kids' movie," Mary Beth said to Andie as they waited for the popcorn and drinks Andie had bought for everyone.

"It's the only one Nathan was allowed to see." Andie handed the clerk a ten-dollar bill. *And Cole*, she added to herself. At home, her friends would have gotten some parent to take them to a PG-13 film. But Mrs. McRae hadn't budged.

Mary Beth reached for Andie's new cowboy hat. "Can I try it on? It's really cool."

Andie nodded, and Mary Beth put it on her own head. "Stick 'em up, pardner," she drawled.

Andie took the cardboard tray of drinks. "Go ahead and wear it. It's making my hair flat."

"O-o-o. You wouldn't want that to happen. Not when you're with *Cole*."

Andie gave her a sharp look. "I am not 'with' Cole."

"Sure, Perez. I see the way you guys look at each other."

"You're crazy," Andie huffed.

161

"Mmm-hmm." Mary Beth cradled the four huge buckets of buttered popcorn in her arms. "I hope Lauren and Jina found good seats."

"They were going to get something close to the back so Cole doesn't have to walk so far," Andie said over her shoulder as she went into the theater.

"Gee, for someone who doesn't like Cole, you sure think about him a lot," Mary Beth teased.

"Oh, shut up." Andie halted in the doorway. It was an old-fashioned theater with velvet-draped walls and a domed ceiling. The lights had dimmed for the start of the show, and it was hard to see.

Jina stood up and waved her arm. Beside her, Andie could see Nathan's cowboy hat silhouetted against the screen. She started down the steep aisle, almost tripping over an empty drink cup.

Lauren sat at the very end, saving two seats. She jumped up and took the buckets of popcorn from Mary Beth.

"Andie wants to sit with Cole," Mary Beth whispered.

"I do not," Andie hissed.

"Yes, you do." Lauren pushed her into the

space in front of the seats. Soda slopped every-where. Andie wanted to kill them both.

"Sit down!" someone yelled.

Feeling herself flush, Andie scooted past the flipped-up seats. When she sat down, she didn't dare look at Cole. He probably thought she *wanted* to sit next to him.

*Well, the jerk was dead wrong.*

She focused all of her energy on ignoring Cole. But it was hard to miss his left leg stretched awkwardly in the cramped aisle. She quickly faced front, concentrating on the movie. She didn't want Cole McRae's con-ceited head to swell as big as his injured knee.

Beside her, Cole chuckled.

*What's so funny?* Andie wondered. It was just a dumb coming attraction.

"Popcorn?" he asked, thrusting the bucket in front of her. Startled, Andie spilled part of her soda.

"Sure!" she replied too loudly. Quickly, she took the container, grabbed a handful of pop-corn, and shoved it in her mouth. *Cool it, Perez,* she told herself. There was no reason why Cole McRae should make her so jumpy.

Taking a napkin, she dabbed at the spilled soda on her leg, then went back to eating popcorn. Cole propped his elbow on the armrest. A few seconds later, he laid his arm along the length of it. Andie chewed slower, eyeing him warily.

He took a drink of his soda, cleared his throat, then shifted closer.

"Uh, Andie," he whispered, "I wanted to—um—say thanks for helping me this afternoon."

"No problem." Andie's cheeks burned. Keeping her eyes glued to the screen, she scooped up some more popcorn.

"And I wanted to apologize."

"For what?"

"I cheated," Cole muttered under his breath.

Andie's hand froze halfway to her mouth, and she twisted to face him. "You *what?*"

Cole glanced awkwardly around. "I cheated," he said again.

"You mean you didn't win the bet fair and square?"

"Well, not totally. I knew which horse to ride."

"*Mom?*"

"Yeah." Nervously, Cole ran his fingers through his tousled hair. "Two years ago I won a million blues on her in trail classes. And in the trail competitions the horse has to clear an obstacle. So I knew she was the best jumper we owned."

Furious, Andie sprang to her feet. "So all this time, you let me and everyone else think you were the best rider. But you cheated! I can't believe it—you, you—" she sputtered. When she couldn't think of a really horrible word, she dumped the bucket of popcorn on his head.

Several people gasped. "Hey!" Nathan hollered. "I wasn't finished eating that!"

Cole calmly brushed the kernels off his shoulder. "You Maryland girls sure do get riled up."

"Sit down up there!" someone yelled.

Andie sat. Beside her Cole was silent. She gulped her soda and watched Cinderella sing to her stupid mice. She should have known Cole would cheat. He was too bigheaded to lose to a girl.

Suddenly she heard Cole choke back a snort of laughter. Andie looked at him suspiciously.

"I guess I deserved that," he told her.

"You bet you did," Andie said. "And you bet

you'd better tell everybody else that you cheated."

"I think they all know now." He grinned sheepishly. Andie's anger dissolved as quickly as it had flared. She couldn't help but smile back.

Picking up her drink, she settled into her seat to watch the movie. Okay, so he apologized and she'd forgiven him—almost. That still didn't mean she liked him.

Hesitantly, Cole reached over and took her hand. "You know, you're really a good rider," he said.

Andie looked at him in surprise, as he laced his fingers through hers.

"For a city slicker," he added, his eyes straight ahead.

"Thanks!" she snapped, trying to pull her hand away. But Cole held tight.

Slowly, Andie relaxed her arm. Her heart was hammering in her chest, and her skin felt warm where it touched his.

On the screen, the cartoon cat cornered the fat mouse. But Andie didn't care. She was trying to remember the last time someone as nice as Cole had held her hand.

*Never?*

Smiling, Andie tightened her fingers around his. She didn't even care if her roommates noticed.

**19**

"I can't believe we haven't found those mares," Cole complained to Andie, Lauren, and Nathan the next morning. Leaning over in the saddle, he rubbed his knee. Andie could tell it was bothering him, but he wouldn't say anything.

"Maybe your mom and dad found them," Andie said, smiling hesitantly at him. Cole gave her a shy smile back. Andie couldn't believe they'd been holding hands last night.

She was riding Dakota and wearing her new cowboy hat with her hair in a braid falling down her back. Lauren wore her new hat, too.

"I'm getting hungry," Nathan complained. "And thirsty. Let's go back to the ranch like Andie suggested. Then we can find out if Mom and Dad found the horses."

Mr. and Mrs. McRae had driven out with Marge and Dorothy. On their way to town, they were going to stop at the neighboring ranches, to see if someone had caught sight of the missing mares.

"Yeah, I guess we better." Reluctantly, Cole reined Crystal toward home. "The problem is yesterday the weather was okay, but tonight the mares might not be so lucky."

Andie glanced up through the bare tree-tops. The sky was sunny and bright, but then she noticed dark clouds rolling in from the east.

"The weatherman didn't say anything about snow," Lauren said.

"Around here a blizzard can hit without warning," Cole explained. "One time, it snowed so hard, a rancher got lost between his barn and his house. He froze to death and he was only fifty feet from his doorstep."

"We've had snow so high it was over my head," Nathan told them.

Lauren frowned anxiously. "Do you think Mary Beth and Jina will get back from cross-country skiing in time? They went to find that line camp you told them about."

"Don't worry, Bronc will pick them up,"

Nathan reassured her in his most grown-up voice. "He's got the snowmobile."

"They shouldn't have gone alone," Andie said. "Why didn't they take Jenny?"

"Mary Beth didn't even tell Jenny," Lauren explained. "She didn't want to get her hopes up. That way, if they find the journal, it will be a surprise."

"The trail to the cabin is pretty easy to follow," Cole added, "*if* they don't get caught in a storm."

Andie glanced worriedly at the darkening sky. As the riders crested a rise, the wind picked up, tossing her hat on to her shoulders.

Cole squeezed Crystal into a jog. "We better hurry. The weather's turning ugly."

Dakota broke into a lope. Andie rocked in the saddle, the sharp wind pelting her cheeks. Ahead of her, Cole twisted, calling over his shoulder, "No matter what happens, stay together!"

Prickles of fear raced up Andie's arms. She glanced over at Lauren. Her friend was holding on to the saddle horn with one hand and clutching her hat with the other. Her eyes were tearing from the icy wind.

The snow started coming down when they

reached the last pasture before home. When Andie caught sight of the barn, she gave a sigh of relief.

Suddenly, she heard a roaring sound, like a train, and the blizzard hit. The wind whipped so hard and fast it almost knocked her from the saddle. With a cry, she grabbed the horn and pulled Dakota to an abrupt halt.

Ahead of her, Cole and Nathan vanished in a blinding cloud of snow. Lauren, who had been right beside her, disappeared.

Andie wiped the snow from her eyes. Dakota turned his tail to the wind. Holding on to her hat, she craned her neck, trying to see the barn—Cole—*anything!*

"Let your horses have their heads!" she heard Cole holler from somewhere.

Andie let the rein go slack. Nudging Dakota with her heels, she urged him forward. Head low, he plowed against the fierce wind.

Andie pulled her scarf over her nose and mouth. The icy flakes stung her eyes so she couldn't see. She clung to the saddle horn, trusting Dakota to find his way to the barn.

"Over here!" Jenny called. Andie peered through her ice-crusted lashes. The older girl stood in the open doorway of the barn, waving her hands. Jenny was only about ten feet away and the barn lights were on, but Andie could barely see her.

Dakota broke into a jog. Andie ducked her head as he hurried into the barn. Lauren was already in the aisle. Cole and Crystal trotted in behind her, leading Nathan's horse.

"Thank goodness you guys were close by when the storm hit!" Jenny exclaimed.

Slowly, Andie dismounted. Her body was trembling with cold.

She flung her arms around Dakota's neck. "Thanks, buddy." He was white with snow and looked more like a polar bear than a horse.

"Did Mary Beth and Jina get back okay?" Lauren asked as she led Mr. Money up the aisle.

Jenny frowned. "I didn't know they'd gone anywhere."

Just then a whirring noise from outside startled the horses, and Bronc zoomed up on a snowmobile. Sliding to a stop, he turned off the motor.

He set his goggles on the top of his head, pulled up his ski mask, and hollered, "Did your friends come back?"

"No!" Andie screamed over the wind. "We

thought you went out to get them!"

"I did! But they weren't at the trail head where they were supposed to meet me. I went up the mountain as far as I could, but then the snow started and I knew I'd better get back."

Andie shot Lauren a horrified look.

"Oh, no!" Lauren cried. "Jina and Mary Beth can't stay out in this storm. You heard Cole's story about the rancher who froze to death. We've got to find them!"

"How much farther do you think the cabin is?" Jina called to Mary Beth.

Mary Beth could hear the worry in her friend's voice. But she didn't slow down to answer.

"Push, glide, push, glide," Mary Beth chanted with each swing of her arms. She was concentrating very hard and she'd finally got the hang of this cross-country skiing stuff. She didn't want to break her rhythm. They'd followed the stream to the gate in the pasture fence. From there, they'd skied uphill for fifteen minutes. If Bronc was right, the cabin was in the ridge of pines ahead. Mary Beth was tired, but she didn't want to quit until they'd reached it.

"Mary Beth!" Jina hollered louder this time. "I've got to stop and rest!"

Mary Beth halted abruptly. Leaning on her poles, she caught her breath.

"This—is—hard—work," Jina gasped.

Mary Beth nodded. Her skin was damp, and she'd unzipped the ski jacket she'd borrowed from Lauren. The morning sun had shone bright, and the effort of skiing uphill had made her hot and sweaty. But as she caught her breath, Mary Beth noticed the chill wind on her cheeks. She glanced up through the pine boughs. The sun had disappeared behind dark clouds.

"Uh-oh," she muttered. "We better hurry and find the cabin."

Jina raised herself up. Her cheeks were covered with sweat, but her chest had stopped heaving. "I think we should go back. Bronc's expecting us at the trail head in twenty minutes. Since it's downhill most of the way, we can make it."

Mary Beth shook her head firmly. "No. The cabin should be just ahead. I don't want to go back without looking for Ellie's journal."

"Why do you *have* to find that journal?"

"I want to help Jenny."

Jina eyed her skeptically. "That's not the only reason."

"You're right." Bending down, Mary Beth brushed snow off her boot. "Everybody laughed at my cattle-rustling theory. I guess I want to prove I'm not a total fool."

"Well, I didn't think you were a 'total' fool," Jina joked. "I mean, there is something weird about a man who wears an eye patch."

"Maybe he's a pirate, hunting for buried treasure on the McRaes' property." Mary Beth laughed. Just then, a big fat snowflake landed on her nose. The girls looked up at the same time.

"Snow!" Jina said gleefully. For a second, they watched the flakes dance and whirl through the green pine needles. In minutes, the snow covered the tops of an outcrop of boulders by the path, turning them into frosted cupcakes. Then the wind began to blow a little harder, and Mary Beth shivered.

"Come on. Let's get to that cabin," she said. Digging her right pole into the snow, she shoved off.

*Push, glide, push, glide.* Mary Beth concentrated on getting her rhythm back. Above her, the pine boughs snapped and creaked.

Suddenly, a deafening howl filled the air, and a blast of snowy wind swooped down the mountain. The force of it hit Mary Beth head-on, sending her flying. Her skis flew out from under her, and she crashed on her back.

Mary Beth struggled to a sitting position as the icy wind tried to push her back down. Her poles dangled from her wrists, and her skis were twisted awkwardly underneath her.

Looking around, Mary Beth squinted her eyes and looked for Jina. But she couldn't see anything except a white curtain of snow. Panic swelled in her chest.

Jina had been right behind her a second ago. Where was she?

Sleet stung Mary Beth's eyes, blinding her. She reached out, feeling around in the snow, trying to find her friend.

"Jina!" she screamed. "Jina! Where are you?"

But the only answer she heard was the howling wind.

**20**

"Jina!" Mary Beth screamed again. What had happened to her? How could she have just vanished?

"Over h—" a muffled cry reached Mary Beth's ears. She turned toward the sound, glimpsing a blur of red. Jina's cap!

Mary Beth crawled through the snow, dragging her skis behind her. Jina sat a few yards away, her arms clasped around her knees. She was hunched over, protecting her face from the biting snow.

"I'm so glad I found you!" Mary Beth sobbed. For a second, the two friends hugged each other, the wind rocking them. Then Jina pointed to their skis.

"We've got to take them off!" she shouted

above the roar of the wind. "We've got to find some protection or we'll be buried."

Mary Beth nodded. She pressed down on her boot clamp with fingers that were numb with cold. Finally, she heard the familiar snap and both her boots were free.

While Jina worked on hers, Mary Beth shielded her face and looked around. Everything was a white blur. She tried to remember what the mountainside had looked like. Were there any rocky ledges to hide beneath? Any thick tangles of brush? Then she remembered the boulders by the side of the path. Her heart beat excitedly. Maybe there was a fissure or some small cave they could crawl into.

"Jina!" She pointed downhill. "Let's try and get to the rocks."

Jina glanced doubtfully in that direction. "How do you know that's where they are? How do you know we won't wander in circles and get lost?"

"I don't! But it's better than sitting here turning into icicles!" Already, their abandoned skis were buried by a layer of snow.

"Okay," Jina agreed. "But we should link our arms and stay together. I don't want to lose you again."

Holding on to each other, the two girls struggled to their feet. The wind was so strong, it slammed Mary Beth into Jina. Her friend grabbed her, then wrapped her arm behind her back. Supporting each other, they floundered through the icy snow.

Mary Beth couldn't see more than a few yards in front of her. But the boulders were huge. How could they miss them? *Hopefully, we're going in the right direction*, she thought miserably.

"There they are!" Jina cried.

Mary Beth shielded her eyes and glimpsed a shadowy hump that looked like a snow-covered elephant. She squeezed Jina's waist encouragingly. Still linked together, the two plowed through a drift.

When they reached the boulders, Mary Beth fell against them. Letting go of Jina, she used the hard surface as a guide and inched her way around. On the other side, two of the rocks met, forming a shallow cave. Inside the hollow, a patch of ground had been swept bare by the wind.

Exhausted, Mary Beth sank under the overhang, resting her back against the rock. Jina dropped down beside her.

"Do you think anyone will find us?" Jina asked nervously.

Mary Beth didn't know what to say. Bronc knew what trail they had taken. But how could anyone find them in a raging blizzard?

"I don't know," Mary Beth said. She smiled encouragingly at Jina. Reaching out, she took her friend's gloved hand and gave it a reassuring squeeze.

"Jina! Mary Beth!" Andie hollered into the wind.

"Jina! Mary Beth!" Lauren echoed her cry. The two rode side by side behind Jenny, who was mounted on Mrs. McRae's horse, Jubilee. They'd changed clothes, tacked up fresh horses, and headed up the mountain to find their friends.

Cole and Bronc had taken horses, too, and gone a different route. Bronc had abandoned the snowmobile, saying, "Horses will find their way home no matter what the weather."

Jenny had warned them to stay right on her tail and next to each other. They all wore blaze orange hunting vests over their coats. Still, if anyone got too far ahead, she was supposed to give a hoot of distress.

As Mom forged through foot-high drifts, Andie searched frantically for any sign of Mary Beth and Jina. It was nearly impossible to see, and almost impossible to hear. The wind had wiped out any signs of tracks. How were they ever going to find Mary Beth and Jina?

Clucking to Mom, Andie rode up next to Jenny.

"Do you think we'll find them?" she hollered.

Jenny shrugged. She'd wrapped a wool scarf around her face. All Andie could see were her eyes, so she couldn't tell if the older girl was discouraged or not.

Pulling the scarf below her mouth, Jenny hollered, "We'll ride to the line camp and rest the horses. Maybe we'll find them there."

She gave Andie the thumbs-up sign, and Andie nodded. Without warning, Mom stopped dead in her tracks. Andie pitched forward, catching her stomach on the saddle horn.

"Ouch. Mom! What was that for?" Andie scolded, too cold to deal with a stubborn horse.

Mom lowered her head and blew at something buried in the snow. Andie leaned sideways, trying to see what it was. A curved blue tip stuck up.

A ski!

"Jenny! Lauren! Mom found a ski!" Dismounting quickly, Andie fell to the ground and started to dig up the ski. She lifted it up. Jenny and Lauren turned their horses to face her.

"It's gotta be one of the skis Jina and Mary Beth wore," Andie told them excitedly. "They must have taken them off. That means they're around here somewhere." Her hopes soared. "We've got to find them!"

Jenny cupped her hand around her mouth. "Or it means they went back on foot to the camp! We'll check there first."

"No!" If Jina and Mary Beth were nearby, there was no way Andie was going to leave them. "We look here first!" Without waiting for Jenny's reply, she started hunting for tracks, more skis, anything that would lead them to her friends.

Mounted on Scooter, Lauren continued to shout their names. Andie made her way downhill, holding on to Mom's mane for support. She stumbled and almost fell. But Mom stopped and waited until she'd regained her balance.

Then, Andie heard it. A faint cry. She froze. Pushing her ski cap away from her ear, she listened again.

"We—ove—ear!"

"It's them!" Dropping Mom's rein, Andie ran toward the cry. "Jina! Mary Beth! Where are you?"

She plowed into a knee-high drift, plunging face first into the snow. Sputtering, she rose up. Jenny rode up behind her.

"Andie, you're going to get lost!"

"But I heard them!"

"I did, too. But don't go running off half crazy."

Andie nodded. Jenny urged Jubilee forward. Lifting her knees high, the mare broke a trail through the drift to a mound of boulders.

Andie caught her breath. Had they taken shelter behind the rocks?

Following Jubilee's path, Andie hurried to the rocks. "Jina! Mary Beth!"

"In here!" A red cap poked from behind a boulder, then a violet one. Andie felt a rush of relief.

"It's them!" she hollered over her shoulder to Lauren and Jenny.

"Are you guys okay?"Andie asked.

"We are now that you're here!" Jina exclaimed as she led the way around the rocks.

Andie gave her friend a big hug. "I can't believe we found you."

"We were about to give up," Mary Beth said, hugging Andie, too. Her cheeks were tear streaked and her freckled face pale.

Andie took Mary Beth's elbow and helped her to the path. "Come on. We can ride double. Jenny says the line camp is just ahead. We can get warm up there."

Slowly, the three girls struggled back to the horses. When Lauren saw them, she had to fight back her tears. Jenny reached down her hand to Jina.

"Grab on. You can ride behind me."

Andie boosted Mary Beth onto Mom, then swung up behind her. When Andie turned Mom back into the wind, the mare didn't even hesitate. Following in a line, the three horses worked their way up the hill.

Fifteen minutes later, Jenny halted to rest the horses. "It should be up ahead," she yelled to the others.

"Don't you know where it is?" Lauren asked.

Jenny shook her head. "I was only there

once. And it's hard to tell in the storm. Everything looks different."

Andie stared over Mary Beth's shoulder. Jenny was right. Everything was a white fog of snow. How would they ever find the camp?

In front of her, Mary Beth moaned. "I'm so cold, Andie. I don't think I can hold on any longer."

Andie tightened her arm around Mary Beth's waist. "Don't worry. I'll keep you from falling."

Andie's fingers and toes were numb, and her teeth were chattering. How much farther did they have to go?

"Do you think we should go back?" Andie asked nervously.

Jenny steered Jubilee around. Jina was clinging silently to her waist.

"It's a half-hour ride back—at least," Jenny said solemnly. "And the horses are beat."

For a moment, everyone stared wordlessly at one another, exhaustion etched on their faces.

*Will we ever find the cabin?* Andie wondered. Jenny thought it was right around the corner. But what if they'd taken the wrong trail? What if they were hopelessly lost in the storm?

Andie glanced over at Jenny. The older girl was peering into the wind. Her brow was furrowed as if she knew they were in trouble, too.

Still, Andie knew they had to do something. They had to find shelter—fast!

Then a piercing whinny rang through the howling wind.

Mary Beth twisted slightly in the saddle. "What's that?" she whispered.

Andie shook her head. "Just the storm." But then she noticed Mom. The old mare's ears were pricked alertly.

Andie tensed. It *wasn't* just the wind. Mom had heard it, too. "Maybe it's Bronc and Cole," she said excitedly.

Mary Beth gasped. "No! It's not Cole or Bronc!" She raised her arm. "Look!"

Andie cupped her hand around her eyes, shielding them from the wind. About ten feet away, a riderless horse galloped into sight. Skidding to a stop, he reared, his front hooves striking the falling flakes.

Andie inhaled sharply, recognizing the horse right away. It was the ghost horse!

**21**

Spinning, the horse bellowed again. Jenny and Lauren swung around. Mom, Scooter, and Jubilee stood rigid, staring at the ghostly sight.

Snaking his head low, the white horse shook his mane as if challenging the group. Then he wheeled and vanished into the pines.

Andie was too stunned to speak.

"See?" Mary Beth blurted. "It wasn't just my imagination. There *is* a ghost horse!"

"Mary Beth, you were right!" Lauren breathed.

"It can't be a ghost horse!" Andie retorted. "That's crazy." Squeezing Mom with her heels, she steered the mare toward the stand of pines. Deep prints marred the snow. "See, I'm right." She pointed at the tracks. "Those were made by a real horse."

"Hey, look!" Mary Beth exclaimed. "It's the line camp!"

Andie jerked up her chin. Sure enough, nestled in a cleared area in the pines was the log cabin.

"We found it!" Mary Beth called to the others. "We found the cabin!"

Jenny and Lauren rode quickly over. Jenny's mouth fell open when she saw the cabin.

"Hurry, let's get the horses into the shelter," she cried, kicking Jubilee into a trot.

The three horses bounded through the snow. Jenny steered Jubilee under a three-sided shelter built against the cabin wall. Mom and Scooter followed right behind.

When Andie dismounted, she sagged against Mom with relief. Every one of her muscles ached. Every inch of bare skin burned from the cold. But they'd made it.

With an exhausted sigh, Mary Beth slid off, too. Andie untied the lead line from the back of her saddle. Then she took the bridle off Mom and hooked the lead to the halter that the horse wore under it. A hitching post ran along the back wall.

"You and Jina go on into the cabin," Jenny directed, handing Mary Beth her saddlebag.

"We've got to rub down the horses."

Andie handed Mary Beth her saddlebag, too. "It's got a couple of granola bars in it."

"Thanks." Mary Beth grinned wearily. "For everything."

When her roommate left, Andie loosened Mom's girth, her thoughts returning to the white horse. *That's who Mary Beth should have thanked*, she thought. Even though the horse had left tracks, it had to be the spirit of Wild Streak.

Because only a ghost horse could have saved their lives.

"Boy, this place smells like dead animal," Mary Beth said, wrinkling her nose. She glanced around the dusty cabin. It was empty except for a table, several chairs, and a few cupboards. There was no electricity, but a window on each side wall allowed in a feeble light. "Can you believe men actually lived here for months?"

Jina was standing by an old wood stove. She stooped to open the door and poked inside. "I'm sure the place was in better shape back then."

"At least it's warmer than outside." Shuddering, Mary Beth slumped in one of the wooden chairs. It tipped over, sending her crashing to the floor in a cloud of dust.

Jina smothered a giggle. "But just as dangerous as being in the storm."

Mary Beth stood up, brushed off her ski pants, and unzipped the jacket. "Actually, now that we're out of that nasty wind, I feel tons better." She set the saddlebags on the table. Opening Andie's, she poked inside, hunting for the granola bars.

"Here." She handed one to Jina.

Just then, Andie, Lauren, and Jenny burst into the room, their boots clomping loudly on the wooden floor.

"What a dump!" Andie announced. "But at least we're out of that blizzard. Whew!" She shook the snow off her cap. "I never want to see snow again in my entire life."

"You'll see it as soon as the storm's over," Jenny said dryly. She dropped down in the other chair.

For the next few minutes, everyone happily munched granola bars and sipped hot chocolate from Jenny's thermos. While Mary Beth chewed, she walked around the cabin, eyeing every nook and cranny. She may have almost frozen to death, but she hadn't forgotten her mission.

Where would Ellie have hidden a journal?

Mary Beth pounced on the cupboards, opening and shutting the doors with loud bangs.

"What are you doing?" Jenny finally asked.

Behind her, Mary Beth heard Jina launch into the explanation of why the two girls had skied up to the cabin in the first place.

"You wanted to find Ellie's journal?" Jenny exclaimed in disbelief.

"Well, you didn't find anything out from the newspaper," Jina said. "And none of the family seem to know—"

Jina went on, but Mary Beth wasn't listening. She was kneeling in front of an old trunk. Slowly, she opened it. Three mice scurried madly about, then darted through a hole in the bottom. Jumping up in alarm, Mary Beth slammed the lid shut.

"Not in there," she declared with a shiver. Then she stared at the back corner of the cabin. A sheet of plywood had been nailed over the log walls.

Mary Beth crossed the room to inspect it. "Why do you think this is here?" She felt

191

around the edges with her fingers.

"Bronc said there used to be a small bedroom off the back," Jenny explained. "But the roof caved in, so they boarded it shut."

Mary Beth whirled to face her. "That's it! I bet that's where the journal is."

"Oh, goody. Now we just need a hammer to pry out the nails," Andie said sarcastically.

"No, we don't. This board is really loose." Mary Beth dug her fingers behind the top section and began to pull.

One side of the plywood sheet gave way with a ripping sound. Jina jumped up and helped her pull the rest from the wall, revealing a doorway leading into a rubble-filled room.

Jina peeked inside. "I can't see much except that it's a mess."

"Well, I'm going to take a look." Cautiously, Mary Beth stepped into the room. She waited for her eyes to adjust to the dark, then poked at the debris with the toe of her boot. Most of the room was blocked off by fallen logs and roofing. Mary Beth knew the odds of finding something were slim. But still...

She lifted up a sheet of tin and kicked her foot underneath. Her toe connected with something that felt softer than a log. Pulling off her gloves, she got down on her hands and knees and felt around. Her fingertips traced a flat, smooth rectangle.

Mary Beth pulled the object into the light. It was a book, bound in old leather. Trembling with excitement, Mary Beth opened to the first page. The book was yellow and half eaten by mice, but she could still read the cursive writing on the title page:

*Journal—Elle McRae—1936*

Mary Beth grinned excitedly. *She'd found it!*

22

*Ellie's Journal—July 14, 1936*
*This cabin is the only place I find peace. Brett is*
*gone from the ranch. Wild Streak is dead. I will*
*never ride or walk again. What is there left for me? I*
*tell Jonathan I want to come up here to paint. But*
*truthfully, I come to this cabin because it was the only*
*place that Brett and I were able to meet...*

"She loved my grandfather!" Jenny exploded out of the kitchen chair. "But how could she? They were related!"

Mary Beth looked up from the journal. She sat cross-legged in the middle of the cabin floor. Her roommates leaned against the side wall of the cabin. Their faces were pale and weary, but they'd been eagerly listening to every word, as she read aloud.

Jenny paced across the room. "They were brother and sister," she said, frowning. She stopped walking and turned to face Mary Beth. "I don't think you should read any more."

"Jenny, it's true they were brother and sister, but Brett was adopted," Jina reminded her.

"Still, it's not right," Jenny said.

"Maybe that's one reason your grandfather left," Lauren suggested. "Maybe he knew it wasn't right, either."

"Maybe." Taking a deep breath, Jenny sat back down. "Go on, Mary Beth. I might as well hear all of it."

*July 15, 1936*
*Bronc brought me to the cabin today. It's been six months since Brett left. I cannot stop crying. I do not wish to live. How could I have known that day would end in such terrible tragedy? Brett told me not to ride Wild Streak. But I took it as a dare. I wanted to defy stuffy old Jonathan. I wanted to show him he can't keep me from the two things I love—Brett and my horses.*

Mary Beth stopped reading and peeked up. Jenny was furiously chewing a nail, but she waved for Mary Beth to continue.

*July 15, 1936—evening*

*I told Bronc to leave me here for the night. There are enough provisions, and he built a fire before he left. Jonathan will be angry, but I don't care. I sit in front of the open stove and see Brett's face in the flames. I hear Wild Streak bellowing to me in the distance. My dear horse is dead. But his spirit is not. It calls to me to tell the truth before I die.*

Mary Beth's voice trailed off. Raising her head, she met Andie's eyes. "So Ellie heard the ghost horse, too."

Andie nodded, for once not protesting. Even Jenny was silent. Ellie's journal had them all in a trance.

"Read!" Lauren urged.

*July 15—night*

*The wind howls outside and I am glad for the comfort of the fire. I have eaten dinner, and now I know I cannot put it off any longer. The truth must be told. Someday, someone will read this journal, perhaps when I am gone. Then the family will know the truth.*

*Brett told Jonathan he was the one who rode Wild Streak and foolishly caused the accident that crippled me. But he wasn't to blame. It was me! Me!*

196

*Riding Wild Streak made me feel wild and free. Brett followed me to make sure I would be safe. We galloped to the cabin, coming upon the wild horses in the valley. I told Brett that Streak and I could catch a pretty mare. He warned me against it, but I took off, chasing the horses with no thought of safety.*

*Then Streak went out of control. He wanted to challenge the stallion for his band of mares. He reared, flipping me to the ground, then raced off to join the wild horses.*

*I was struck unconscious and when I came to, there was no feeling in my legs. Even so, when Brett brought me down from the mountain, Jonathan would not speak to us. Weeks later, Wild Streak was shot by Mustang rustlers. The stallion had been Jonathan's hope for the future of the ranch and I had lost him.*

*It wasn't until much later, after I was stronger, that I learned that Brett had claimed all responsibility for the accident and losing Wild Streak. Jonathan turned his full fury on Brett and banished him from the ranch forever.*

"So it wasn't Brett," Jenny whispered.

Mary Beth stopped reading and glanced up. Tears were streaming down the older girl's cheeks. Mary Beth didn't blame her. Not only was Ellie's story horribly sad, but all this time,

197

her grandfather had been blamed for something he didn't do.

"There's more," Mary Beth said.

Jenny wiped away tears. "Go ahead."

*By then it seemed too late to tell the truth. Brett was gone. I was crippled. My letters east went unanswered. I do not know where Brett is. I don't know if he still loves me, but I do know that I will always love him. Perhaps, one day, he will know how much.*

Mary Beth turned to the next page. It was blank. Sighing loudly, she closed the book. Lauren sniffled to herself. Andie and Jina sat in dazed silence.

"That was so romantic!" Lauren choked out. "And so sad."

Mary Beth nodded and peered over at Jenny. The older girl's eyes brimmed with tears. "Now I know what really happened," Jenny whispered. "Thanks for finding the journal, Mary Beth. You never gave up."

Mary Beth smiled sadly. Then a beam of sunlight that shot through the window made her blink. "It's stopped snowing!"

Everyone jumped up and ran to the window, shouting with joy. Mary Beth and Jina

Jina, Andie, Lauren, and Mary Beth—the four roommates in Suite 4B at Foxhall Academy— may not see eye to eye on everything. But they do agree on one thing: they *love* horses! You'll want to read all the books in this extra-special series.

Eliza, Lisa, Molly, and Abby are more than just great friends. They all love animals—and hate to see them in trouble. So they've started their very own club:

# THE ANIMAL RESCUE SQUAD

Don't miss any of their fun adventures!

*The Black Stallion*
*The Black Stallion and Flame*
*The Black Stallion and Satan*
*The Black Stallion and the Girl*
*The Black Stallion Legend*
*The Black Stallion Mystery*
*The Black Stallion Returns*
*The Black Stallion's Blood Bay Colt*
*The Black Stallion's Courage*
*Son of the Black Stallion*
*The Young Black Stallion*

# Camp Zombie

## by Megan Stine & H. William Stine

### *The living dead rule at...*

### Camp Zombie

What's worse than being stuck at camp with a bunch of rotten counselors? Being stuck at camp with *dead* rotten counselors! That's what happens to Corey Campbell, who realizes he's in danger of becoming zombie chow!

### Camp Zombie: The Second Summer

In this spine-tingling sequel to the best-selling *Camp Zombie,* it's up to Corey and his sister, Amanda, to save their unsuspecting cousin Griffen from the evil Brian. He may have been a nasty camp counselor, but now he's a *terrifying* zombie!

### Camp Zombie 3: The Lake's Revenge

When their grandparents' RV breaks down beside an all-too-familiar lake, Corey, Amanda, and Griffen know they are in for *major* trouble. Especially when last summer's living-dead campers emerge from the murky depths! But the worst is yet to come—Amanda and Corey must race to put plan Zombie-Rescue into action when Griffen gets zombified. The world's scariest camp just keeps getting scarier!

BULLSEYE BOOKS PUBLISHED BY RANDOM HOUSE, INC.

# WANNA CHILL?

### Check out the horror series
## ZODIAC CHILLERS

| DUE DATE | | |
|---|---|---|
|  |  |  |
|  |  |  |
|  |  |  |
|  |  |  |
|  |  |  |
|  |  |  |
|  |  |  |
|  |  |  |
|  |  |  |
|  |  |  |
|  |  |  |
|  |  |  |
|  |  |  |